With Love

and

Peace

Chocolate

*Book has been handcrafted from cover to cover,
including the watercolor illustrations by Carolee.*

Navigating the Potholes of Life

*Dedicated to David
for his unending courage
as he journeyed
to his eternal reward.*

To:

_____

_____

From:

_____

_____

Acknowledgments

To all my friends and family who willingly gave of their time to edit the stories of my twelve books; patiently taught me computer jargon; shared their computer skills with InDesign, Photoshop and GIMP and guided me through the copyright, ISBN and barcode maze. I couldn't have done it without you.

Navigating the Potholes of Life

ISBN: 978-1-947573-09-3

Library of Congress Catalog Card Number: 2017911879

The Carolee Collectables
Printed in the United States of America
www.crystalsforkids.org

Carolee O'Neill
http://books2c4kids.com

Make Life a Melody

And

Sing every Refrain

Navigating the Potholes of Life

Chapter 1

Remembrances of the past plunged to the hollowness of my soul. The pain of it was hidden, like the depths of the canyon hugging the shores of Monterey Bay. The azure waters of the Pacific kept their secret. Mine would be held silently within. A safe harbor—a moment of peace for my spirit's quest, but where? How could I escape the demon that rode the tides of my life? Emotions dug deep as I attempted to deal with the horrid images that plagued my mind, images of David dying with a rare form of Lou Gehrig's disease. Most of the time I felt weary, sick to my stomach, and with an urge to try to outrun my thoughts.

Fall held the deep blue of the sky in its grip when a friend suggested that I shouldn't be alone over the forthcoming holidays. At the very least I should rent a place in a warmer climate.

Remembering her words, I realized I could stay a month with my daughter in Tucson, Arizona, and then rent a park model at The Voyageur RV resort for a month. It seemed like a workable plan, so I began making the arrangements.

I loved the Superstition Mountains that lay a little north of Tucson. Perhaps a drive through them might allow me to honor a memory or two and bring some peace to my troubled soul. It would be the perfect place to clear my mind.

As I needed seclusion, the trip to the mountains became foremost in my mind. I'd drive north as soon as I could be settled in Tucson.

Carolee O'Neill

A week after I arrived at my daughter's home, I left for Canyon Lake in the Superstition Mountains. Standing by the water, I stared toward the horizon as the breeze touched my face and moved tenderly through my hair. I watched as the sunlight played leapfrog over the crests of waves, carrying hues of blue and brown toward the rocky bank. Bathed by gentle waves, the napping shoreline reflected its amber depths. A distant speedboat insulted the silence, sending swells crashing noisily against the shore. Then silence returned, and peace once again calmed my soul.

As I breathed in the ambiance, children in brightly colored swimsuits burst from a caravan of cars. Mothers hurried after them laden with toys, inner tubes, and towels. With sheer delight, the children ran to the lake and stopped quickly when their tiny toes touched the snow-chilled water. They giggled, swirled the water with their feet and then proceeded, without regard for the icy temperature. Grating sounds surrounded me as other children dug their shovels into the stony bank and emptied the content into buckets that stood lop-sided on the rocky shoreline. Driven by the simplicity of their lives, silence filled only the spaces between the children's intermittent screeching. I lingered for a short time in this beautiful spot and then went on, refreshed with the joy that only children can bring to your soul.

Chapter 2

Even though it had been eight months since David died, the silence of driving back to Tucson from Canyon Lake caused the past to spring into my mind like a panther leaping upon its prey. I needed to think of ways to break this pattern and get back to the joy. A quick stop might help me focus on something like the beauty of the setting sun pampering the quiet evening with its vibrant hues. e.

I pulled over to the side of the road, stepped out of the car and took a deep breath. The fresh mountain air felt cool to my lungs. I began to stroll along the roadside, gazing into the depths of a canyon polka-dotted with green shrubs and saguaro cacti. The sun had begun to hide behind the rusty colored mountains, casting shadows of gray and black on the desert sand. I kicked a stone and watched it tumble into the brush. It had been a beautiful day, warm for the mountains, but it was gone just like the stone. Thoughts of David's final days bounced my mind from reality to denial. Allowing myself to be haunted wouldn't lead me into the future. I needed to change my attitude and get involved in something that would thrust me back into living.

A smile crossed my lips as I remembered the dent toward the top of our thirty- eight foot fifth wheel. David's casual attitude led me to believe I should forget about it. "Must have come from one of those truck mirrors," he had said. Horrified, I asked, "The ones that are attached to the trucks?" It didn't seem funny at the time, but now it would be a cherished memory.

Car lights flashed from around a curve. The car swerved and pulled off the road, parking in front of me. "You OK?" a man hollered.

A shiver surged through my body. I realized how insane it would seem to see someone walking around in the desert alone.

"Yes, thank you. I'm just enjoying the view."

"I wouldn't hang around these parts too long after the sun goes down, ma'am. There are a lot of wild animals in these mountains. Besides, the road gets pretty tricky after dark."

"Thank you," I hollered back. "I'll be careful."

He waved and was gone in a flash.

Tricky, he said. I can't imagine towing a fifth wheel up, down and around these curves, but I'm not sure David wouldn't have tried it. Driving our little twenty-six foot fifth wheel had been such a treat. Everything fell into place when we bought it, as it was meant to be. Maybe the future will fall into place just as nicely.

Now I wanted to feel, remember the goodness of the day, the warmth of the sun, the brilliance of the stars. I felt alive! Light filled my life, not darkness. Hadn't I just experienced it this day? It had been a grand time, the waves lapping at the shore, the children with their buckets, the moments of silence. I wished I could've stayed there forever, but that only happens in fairy tales.

Chapter 3

After the holidays I moved into the park model as planned. Palm trees accented by flood lights, flower beds and real grass adorned the entrance to the RV resort. The streets were filled with seniors going to or from the many activities The Voyageur sponsored. I decided to join something that would fill my life with light and not the darkness that haunted me day and night, without a tear. So I went to the activity department and read their brochures.

The morning exercise class would be just the thing to clear my head and start the day off with a fresh start. Bound to keep up with people who were older than I was and moving much better, I did my one-two-three-fours and stretches. All I could think of was how much pain they caused.

Hearing me moan, the fellow behind me said, "It'll get better after awhile. Just stick with it."

I smiled and thought—but will I survive?

Before class the fellows would gather, sharing war stories about their rigs. I had considered owning a motor home, but being alone, I discounted the idea. Yet, the memories of David and my son Chris talking about their adventures as they panned for gold, began to revive my interests. Likewise, the fellows' conversations gave my dream another boost. Here stood a golden opportunity to move forward with my life and learn something about motor homes, with no strings attached. Life passed quickly and I didn't want to waste another moment.

I inched my way between the brawny, six-foot fellows who towered over me by eight inches. When conversation waned within the group, I'd raise a question or two and tell them about my make-believe dream. Spurred by their macho nature, most of the fellows were anxious to answer my questions. After all, it wasn't every day they met a mature woman who might actually buy a motor home.

When I wasn't talking to the fellows about their rigs, I rode my mountain bike through the motor home section, reminiscing about past travels. One afternoon, a Pleasure Way van passed me. Its glossy white exterior glistened as the sunlight glanced off its nineteen-foot side.

Wondering what it looked like inside, I decided to find out. I began my pursuit.

The fifteen mile an hour speed limit should keep it in view. Nevertheless, it took every ounce of energy I could muster to keep up.

Questions popped into my head as I shifted gears and pedaled faster than I knew possible.

Now there's something I could handle. I wonder how much that costs. It doesn't look like it would have enough storage space. The gas mileage has to be better than the Class A's or even the Class C's for that matter. Whatever I considered, I'd have to be able to do it on social security and the small pension David left me. That might be tough.

The van made a right turn several streets ahead. Concerned I'd lose it, I pedaled harder. When I rounded the corner, I saw it pull into a driveway at the far end of the street. In spite of my legs begging for relief, I continued my pace. I wanted to arrive at the home before the folks went inside. Hardly able to catch my breath, I pulled into their driveway.

These folks are going to think I'm crazy or else the most brazen woman in the world.

An elderly lady, with a curious smile, slid out of the driver's side as I dismounted my bike. Returning the smile, I noticed an impish gleam in her eyes. Gentle lines embraced the smooth skin on her face as she stood fiddling with the keys in her hand. The passenger's door opened. The sight of a cane emerged, followed by a gentleman with a quizzical look on his face.

I introduced myself and told them I had lost my husband and I was looking for a way to move forward with my life. The lady's interest sparked when I told her I was impressed with their unit. She offered to give me a tour. Walking through the coach, I remembered David's words. I'd need something bigger, especially if I planned to live in it for five or six months out of the year.

After the tour I listened to Esther tell me her story. For years this agile, bright-minded, eighty-year-old lady had been driving their coach back and forth from Washington State to Tucson, Arizona, with her invalid husband. Inspired by her example, the idea of following my dream seemed like a possibility.

The months that followed were filled with learning about motor homes of all sizes and shapes. I had a reason to dream, to plunge forward into the future and travel the country. Vibrant meadows

7

where antelope grazed would capture my gaze. I could stand in awe of rugged, snow-packed peaks that released their crystal waters in the glimmer of the sun. I could hear the azure waters of the Pacific call my name through the whispering wind. A loving Father had placed the future in my hands and I wanted to grab it.

Chapter 4

By the end of my stay at The Voyageur, I had scrutinized a variety of coaches like the Lazy Daze, Roadtrek, Holiday Rambler, Jayco, and Minnie Winnebago. Each one gave me a better idea as to what I'd need to be comfortable.

Class A motor homes probably wouldn't work for me. The Greyhound-bus-like windshield enveloped the greater portion of the front of the vehicle, striking my chords of vulnerability. I imagine flying in a helicopter over the Grand Canyon would give me the same queasy sensation. After a quick search on the Internet, I found there was a limited number of pre-owned Class C's on the market; I'd have to give the Class A's a good hard look.

Well, I tried. I really did, but every time I sat in the driver's seat of a Class A, I felt like I was in a fish bowl.

I began looking for reasons not to buy anything, like there wasn't a door by the driver seat most of the time. I'd have to go to the stairwell on the opposite side of the coach to exit. A tad eccentric, but not for my age group. It could be that I just didn't want to walk across the coach to get out. Salespeople told me I'd get used to the windshield and the missing door.

I wasn't convinced. There would be enough of an adjustment, learning to take care of a rig by myself. An overwhelming factor emerged when I stood next to its Greyhound bus size and looked up and up and up. My RV brush would never reach that far. It was too much scrubbing for me.

Class A

As I continued to explore different units the facts became clear. Amenities had to be listed before I could be sure I would get what I wanted. No matter what coach I chose, there would be some concessions, but right now I wanted it all.

Every morning before exercise class the fellows listened to my adventures from the previous day. They laughed with gusto, saying I had conned people into showing their units with my smile. I didn't mind the teasing. After all, they were offering a free crash course. They knew whatever I needed to learn, even when it came to towing a car.

One of the guys, with a chubby bulldog face, said, "You're going about this motor home thing all wrong. You need to find yourself a man who owns one. Then you can leave the worries to him."

A smirk crossed my face, "No thanks, been there, done that. This is going to be my baby."

His chin dropped to the floor and bounced back up again before he said, "You mean you're not interested in a little hanky-panky?"

"Sorry," I said as I attempted to control the giggle that had caught in my throat.

Strange, this whole idea had started as a game that hid itself below the surface of my consciousness. A fun game, but it kept me blind to the seeds I had planted. There wasn't any pressure to actually buy a motor home, until I inadvertently told my family and friends.

"You're going to do what?" they whispered in amazement, eyes bulging.

With that, I felt like someone had slapped me into reality. Blindness vanished. The stage for ownership had been set or would it be unset.

My daughter couldn't believe I could entertain such an idea. She expressed concern about my being on the road alone, coupling it with the violent ways of the world. That caused more seeds of uncertainty to flow. After some sleepless nights and a knot in my stomach, the one I had just gotten rid of after losing David, I had to question my dream. The pressure was on and my game had pushed its way into reality.

Chapter 5

The next couple of days were spent organizing and packing my belongings for the trip back to Indiana. As it was, I had moved four times since I left home, so things never seemed to be where I remembered putting them. With each move items had to find a new spot, another shelf, a different room. Memory was taking its good-natured time in catching up to their locations. After I finished packing I turned my attention to the car. The tires needed to be replaced and the muffler had developed a hole.

I didn't waste any time getting home. Heading east blessed my day with breathtaking sunrises; whereas driving late allowed me glimpses of sunsets in the side and rearview mirrors. I arranged food and water on the seat next to me so I could continue, stopping only for gas, nature and a good stretch.

The roads were decent most of the way. There was some construction, but there's always some construction. At least the weather kept its senses much better than the trip out to Arizona.

Torrential rains, from a nearby tornado, had thrown buckets of water at my windshield. Barely visible, trucks emerged on the other side of the median from a heavy mist, like ghosts creeping out of their graves. All that water coming from trucks so far away didn't seem possible.

After more miles than I cared to drive in that cloudburst, I decided not to struggle against Mother Nature any longer. I took the next exit and pulled into a McDonald's. Of course I couldn't use my umbrella without becoming Mary Poppins. So I stayed put. The smell of French fries teased my olfactory glands in spite of the rain. In thanksgiving, I asked God to bless the boring stuff sitting in my cooler.

The storm had worn itself to a drizzle in about forty-five minutes. Before I ventured down the road, I needed a bathroom. I made a dash for the side door of McDonald's, getting another whiff of French fries. I ignored the aroma the best I could, telling myself I had plenty of healthy morsels in my tummy.

As I drove, thoughts of buying a motor home continued to graze on the spirited part of my mind. Silence had become the vehicle that gave my thoughts the opportunity to paint visions of green forests and snow-capped mountains. The passion surged though my veins as if I were riding a ten foot wave off the windward coast of Maui. It would be a big step, especially so soon after losing David.

I could sell the house and travel for awhile, but then I wouldn't have any roots. That probably wouldn't be too smart.

Probably being a bit zealous. In nursing I told folks that after losing a loved one, a person should wait at least two years before making any major decisions. With time deleting the moments of my life I didn't want my limited future put on hold for that long.

By the time I reached Indiana, few doubts remained. My dream had become an addiction. Pursuing the idea, I'd have a different kind of folks

13

in my life, folks like the ones who took the time to share their tidbits about owning a motor home. Their faces gleamed as they recited their tales of woe, turning them into incredible memories. Folks like the fellows who told me anything I wanted to know, sometimes under the direction of their wives.

Three and a half days later I drove into my garage. As soon as the sheets were off the furniture and the house freshened, I headed for Barnes and Noble. There I wandered the aisles reviewing books like "The RVer's Bible: Everything You Need to Know About Choosing, Using, Enjoying Your RV" by Kim and Sunny Baker, "How to Buy an RV Without Getting Ripped Off" by D. Gallant.

I spent so much time browsing I'm sure the staff thought I'd set up camp.

The reference librarian, a slender middle-aged woman with puffy eyes, would be my next resource. She supplied me with literature that made the quest more interesting. After all this research, I felt sure I had all my ducks in a row. However, my knowledge base wasn't on any more solid ground than a boat in a swamp. As the saying goes, the more you think you know, the more you need to realize how little you know.

See Appendix 1: "Want List."

The "want" list I developed was put into categories—Coach, Chassis, Amenities, and Miscellaneous. This made the job of compiling my necessities for a dealer pretty simple.

Next, I had to know what motor homes cost. I remembered that David had listed the fifth wheel under our Good Sam membership. I checked my billfold and found his old membership card, and it hadn't expired. I called the number on the card and the gentleman told me how to find the recreational vehicles listed with Good Sam.

Preferring a Class C, the search began there. Then I searched NADA and the Kelley Blue Book for their fair market value. The features that were "musts," like a generator, slide-out, and hydraulic jacks were included in the search. They would add to the value of the coach when it came to resale. The coach would have to be self-contained. I wanted all the comforts of home, regardless of whether I got plugged in or not. I planned on convenience, even when parked at places like WalMart and Flying J's, never inconvenience. The hydraulic jacks, for instance; would keep me from living in a lopsided, caddy-wampum coach.

Crawling under the coach every time it needed leveling was not a lady-like maneuver, so I thought.

On the Internet I explored the costs of motor homes, the availability of different units and the different styles. They were all at my fingertips.

Chapter 6

After a few hours of surfing the net, sit-itis set in. There were hundreds of used coaches across the country. Buying a new camper wouldn't be cost-effective. I didn't want to pay the sticker price for a new unit and watch it depreciate by thousands of dollars overnight; nor did I want to absorb the toxic chemicals that were emitted from the glue, the carpet, and the furniture.

Then my addiction led me to what I thought were greener pastures. I seriously consider a unit right outside of Tucson. After many long distance conversations with a salesman, it dawned on me that the green in my pastures wasn't ready for harvest. Buying something so far away? Why, I had never hooked up a sewer hose or backed up a unit. In fact, I had never driven a motor home, and I was thinking about driving over twenty-two hundred miles across the country by myself? My obsession had captured my sanity. I needed to take a trip back to reality.

Having zero experience, I got a bright idea. I could go to the dealership that sold us our fifth wheel and talk them into letting me drive a motor home. As I'm so good at getting my way with my smile, I thought I'd put it to the test. Surprised as a toad's hair split in two, it worked. They didn't let me drive far, but I still got the feel of a thirty-one foot camper. Round and round I went in the Hart City's parking lot. I made some right and left turns and backed it up a couple of times. The salesman said I was a natural. Obviously, he thought I'd fall for that line. Of course, it did dilute some of the panic running through my veins and the trip around the lot really made me feel like a pro.

Are you laughing yet?

Having a feel for the market, my next step would be financing. In the process, I discovered that being a real estate broker was more of a handicap than an asset. I knew enough about interest rates and payments to put my nerves on a roller coaster ride. To top it off, my securities were at the bottom of a bear market.

The loan officer, who tried to be nice, made the mistake of telling me I could ask all the questions I wanted. I had plenty, so many that her polite smile turned into a grimace. This change in attitude gave me the feeling that one more question might cause my evacuation. However, persistence paid off. A Home Equity loan would give me another exemption on the house, lowering my taxes.

I needed to check with Edward Jones to make sure the dividends would cover the payment, without touching the principle. My agent confirmed my calculations. The plan would work. The monthly payment would be made right to the lending institution from my account.

By the end of May 2002, I presented my wish list to twenty RV dealerships. I delivered the list myself to the salespeople I knew from my fifth wheel days. The others were mailed after I had gathered names and addresses from the yellow pages, the Internet, and an RV magazine that was circulated in my area.

Working toward my goal, I got the impression the salespeople didn't want to overextend themselves.

Coffee in hand, they'd walk around waiting for a deal to fall into their laps. When I gave them my list they chuckled saying, "You'll never find a unit that matches everything you want unless you buy something new."

The time was ripe in spite of their comments. The new coaches would be hitting the market in July, making the present models a year older. Current owners of motor homes would be trading up. The market would be well-stocked with used units.

Once I discovered the attitude of the salespeople, I tried a little gentle persuasion. I told them I could buy a coach right from an owner on the Internet. Miraculously, a coach became available and most of the criteria had been met, a thirty-one-and-a-half foot, top of the line, Ultra Supreme by Gulf Stream. It only had 7,300 miles on the odometer and it was as clean as a whistle.

All I had to sacrifice was the interior color scheme, but the condition of the coach convinced me to forego my desire for an almond color scheme. The gunmetal blue enhanced this classy chassis just fine.

Shaking in my boots, I signed the contract and accepted the blessing. Adventure would be mine right after the day of closing.

Chapter 7

Thoughts of the closing urged my adrenals into action. The thrill of owning a coach began to dissipate. I've never been a gambler. I couldn't purchase a blouse without sliding into buyer's remorse.

Since childhood the sound of money jingling in my piggy bank was sweet music to my ears. Spending mega-dollars on a motor home would diminish this tune. My rumbling, knotted stomach returned along with more sleepless nights. I wondered if I'd ever get out of the bathroom.

Refiguring finances became a daily routine. I wished that David could help me, but he wasn't available. I remember telling the fellows at exercise class, "this is my baby." So technically I asked for it.

A meager attempt to console my nervous system burst forth.

Remember, you're the one who loves to solve problems and make things come together. You're a thinker, a survivor, not a quitter.

When I shared my dream people marveled at my courage. They said they would never be brave enough to attempt such a feat, especially with a hearing disability.

My false pride swallowed this hook, line, and sinker. All the compliments convinced my ego I stood on terra firma. Well, it didn't take long before pride turned to humility. Unfortunately, it happened in the wee hours of the morning.

That's when the "aha's" arrived. Aha, there's a big difference between doing something and watching it being done. Aha, I didn't have to buy anything. Aha, I could do like the man in the exercise class suggested—find me a man—oh no, don't think that one would work.

Being a real estate broker I should've remembered I could've rescinded the contract. During my waking hours, none of this dawned on me. All this brilliance went on vacation as soon as I signed on the dotted line.

The things David handled covered a wide range, letting me know, for sure, I didn't know what I didn't know! The literature was full of stories about the slide not coming in, jacks not going up or the refrigerator not converting to gas. Those were "no biggies" for David, but I would revert into a stage ten panic attack.

With the slide, he would've hand-cranked it into position or jumped it with our cables. I've never jumped a car, but I was sure I could learn, probably at a very inconvenient time. I'd have to be careful with the generator. If I didn't hear the motor turn over when I pushed the starter, I could grind the gears. No, I didn't have the muscles to do the heavy duty work on the camper. Most fellows don't either.

Have you ever seen a tire on a camper?

With all the planning, I admit I hadn't spent enough time on the "what ifs." What I wanted in a motor home had taken priority. Then again, if I paid too much attention to the mechanical end of the coach, maybe my dream would've been lost. I had gotten myself on the merry-go-round of travel and I didn't want to get off. I had a lot to learn, but I didn't see that as a reason to abandon my dream.

Chapter 8

Working with my real estate clients, taught me that closings brought starry-eyed and overly agreeable clients to the table. Being on my own with the purchase of the camper and not thinking as well as I'd like, I needed to expand my list to include the maintenance, an understanding of the different fluid levels, especially the jacks, and how to winterize the unit. This should keep me focused.

David had trouble with the winterizing process, so I wanted some detailed instructions. As the coach was a couple of years old, the potential for problems was there. Pencil and paper a breath away, I jotted down things I needed to remember.

See Appendix 2: Owners Absentee List to Prepare the Home.

Diverting my attention to lists and tasks didn't stop time from passing. As closing approached, little jabs of adrenaline shocked my body every time my mind whispered *motor home.* My nerves felt like tangled ganglions bunched into a snowball that was rolling down a hill, gaining momentum.

Mr. Jack Snagg, the salesman who wrote the contract, called the first week of July. Everything was set for eleven in the morning on July 15, 2002. Upon arriving at the dealership, I would inspect the coach with the assistance of one of their pre-delivery staff. Once I approved the coach, I would complete the paperwork for the transaction. I had done my homework so I should be all set.

Regardless, tingles were spreading from my stomach to the wee corners of all four limbs. I told myself to—*cool it!* That didn't work. I felt like I had put myself at the edge of a fifty foot diving board. Only time would tell if I'd land on my feet, like the proverbial cat.

The dealership at Richmond, Indiana, was at least 180 miles from my home. I would need to find someone to drive me there so I could bring the coach home. I considered towing the car as an option. As jumpy as I had been about the whole transaction, how did I ever come up with this as a possibility?

After several calls with negative responses, Mr. and Mrs. Chuck Clover, some of David's elderly cousins, said they would be glad to take me. The couple lived in a small town about an hour's drive from my home. I asked if they'd like to spend the night with me, but Mary said, no. They were used to getting up early so it wouldn't be a problem.

The weatherman predicted a hot, muggy day as Mary and Chuck drove into my driveway. Upon seeing their car, I pulled the front door closed and looked skyward. A haze hung on the distant horizon.

The black Honda Civic cruised easily down the highway with Mary behind the wheel and me in the passenger's seat. Chuck, her elderly husband, sat crosswise in the back seat. The space scrunched his tall, lean frame, making it impossible to sit comfortably. Mary, a pleasingly plump lady with a smile for the world, always kept the speed limit.

As we traveled south, the hood of the car reflected the brilliance of the westward sun. Mary squinted as she pulled the visor down to shield her eyes.

Every mile seemed to move us further from our destination as we dilly-dallied through numerous small towns, keeping the speed limit. As much as I wanted to be driving, I knew Mary's calm nature was better behind the wheel than someone who exhibited the attention span of a five-year-old. Anxiety planned on being my companion for the day. Mary and Chuck would be my captive audience as I talked too much.

We arrived at the dealership at ten forty-five in the morning, fifteen minutes before my appointment. The short walk from the car to the office building seemed long in the heat. Perspiration made its own river off my forehead and down the back of my neck. Mary's face was flushed; Chuck lumbered along behind her, pausing to wipe his brow with his handkerchief.

As I opened the door to the dealership, welcome relief greeted us from the central air. I sneezed from the smell of new tires.

Directly in front of us was a line of new thirty and forty-foot, Class A motor homes. As far as I could see, they were two, maybe three rows deep, and they reached from wall to wall. Dollar signs flashed in my head. I felt outclassed financially as I compared my Class C to the mammoth price tags these coaches demanded. A café in front of the motor homes invited the customers to sit and have a cup of coffee while they spent their thousands. Some salesmen were gathered conversing, while others were sitting at the tables.

A lady, with too much rouge on her round face, sat behind a chest high partition that enclosed a desk. She asked my name and then directed us to the waiting room in a building across the street for closing. Confused by her comment, I told her I needed to inspect the unit first. She wiggled on her wide bottom that had sat too many years, and told me they would take care of me across the street.

I tried to maintain a happy attitude. However, my background in real estate coupled with my past experience with RV dealerships, told me to get my head out of the sand. I glanced at Mary and Chuck as I turned to leave the building.

Mary had a little smirk on her face as she said, "I'm not the least bit surprised."

Stepping outside, the cool air that had bathed our bodies quickly dissipated. I could see loveseats and RV tires standing inside the front corner windows as we approached the building.

Opening the door, the contrast between the heat and cold made the air feel frigid. Bins of toilet paper arranged around the checkout counter tempted the customer with their savings. Rows of carefully stocked shelves stood in a line and held everything from chemicals to can openers to twelve volt curling irons. A fifty foot walk took us through the RV store to the waiting room. Entering, I noticed a young woman seated behind a desk to my left. With the change in plans foremost in my mind, I directed my comments to the young woman as politely as my escalating ire would allow.

"I was told I'd be inspecting the unit before closing. Now the clerk across the street said I will be closing first. Why would I buy something without seeing it? That wouldn't be very smart now, would it?"

With a quick glance at my face, the receptionist asked my name and grabbed the phone.

"I'll call your salesman," she said.

Seeing that Mary and Chuck had taken a seat, I crossed my arms and plunked down in the hard chair next to Mary.

Cool grays and solid blacks were the basic colors used to decorate the stark room. The chairs, with an institutional flare, were thinly padded. In the center of the room a smaller group of chairs surrounded a coffee table covered with magazines.

When Mr. Snagg, my salesman, entered the waiting room, no pleasantries were exchanged. Seeing Mary and Chuck, but not acknowledging them, he said in his southern Indiana drawl, "If you want to inspect the coach first, you'll have to wait until someone has time to do that. Right now we have you scheduled to close first."

"That isn't what you promised me."

As he walked out of the room, his eyes were expressionless, his voice a monotone, "Regardless. That's the way it's set up."

Mortified, I mumbled, "Why, he didn't even make an effort to see if anything could be done about it."

I wanted to grab him by the shirt collar, like a mother would a rowdy child. But I wasn't thinking fast enough to attack his lack of manners. My great words of wisdom usually come in the middle of the night. That's when I can construct my rebuttal into powerful sentences and deliver them with the fires of hell attached.

Look here, buddy, we just drove over one hundred and eighty miles through tons of small towns to keep an appointment which you goofed up. We've been on the road for hours and all you can say is 'that's the way it's set up'? The ball isn't in your court, wise guy. Maybe losing the sale would get your attention!

Relishing the power of my words, my brain groaned the thoughts I delivered into thin air.

This time his smug attitude had me wanting to cancel the appointment. I could come back at a later date, but I knew that wouldn't work. Who would give me a ride a second time? I couldn't expect Mary and Chuck to do it. Besides, the chances are I'd end up with the same scenario. Mr. Snagg had put me in a squeeze play, calling my bluff. He probably figured I'd relinquish my "inspection wants" to accommodate the Clovers. Wrong! His attitude had robbed us of our time, poorly represented the dealership and consequently played out as an insult to the Clovers and to myself.

The receptionist sat staring wide-eyed, sure I would slam-dunk her at any second. After a moment, she turned her attention to a schedule that lay on her desk. Her finger drew a line from the middle of the page down.

She replied quietly, "I don't have an opening until after 1:00 this afternoon, ma'am."

Mary and Chuck glanced back and forth at each other, smiling. Mary told me to take a deep breath. She said my face and neck were a bright crimson. The dreamy nights spent contemplating green meadows and trickling streams had turned into a mud slide. The message from Mr. Snagg was clear. He had the sale. Whatever happened to me, tough! Not willing to let my dream be squashed, I remembered a piece of advice my grandma gave me many years ago.

"Stick to your guns, Sweetheart, especially if you think someone hasn't been fair."

I decided to do just that.

Turning to the Clovers, "I'm really sorry about this delay, but I can't buy a unit without seeing it first."

"Don't worry about it," Mary said. "We don't blame you one bit. It seems that's the way business is done these days. You do whatever you have to."

"Thanks, Mary. I guess we might as well go for lunch. At least we can take care of something while we're waiting."

Chapter 9

After lunch we drove back to the dealership. The sweltering heat continued its unceasing blows as we walked toward the building. Again, I felt the welcomed coolness as we walked through the RV store to the waiting room. Before sitting down next to Mary, I picked up a magazine from the pile on the table. Seeing her engrossed in her reading, I decided to relax and try to stay calm. I couldn't make things happen any faster by fretting.

In spite of my good intentions, I continued to glance at the clock. I've never been particularly good at waiting. Often, as a youth, I sat in the car for hours while my dad finalized a business transaction. That had a dimming effect on my ability to be patient. And it always seemed to happen on the coldest or the hottest days.

When it got to be two in the afternoon, my concern grew with each movement of the minute hand. Every time an individual entered the room, my eyes averted from the paragraph I had already read twenty times, hoping the next person coming in would ask for me.

A few minutes later, a well-tanned and well-endowed blonde approached the receptionist's desk with a clipboard in hand. The receptionist pointed in our direction.

The young woman extended her hand as she walked toward me. "Hello, I'm Sally. I'll be taking you through your motor home and answering your questions."

I introduced myself and the Clovers. Then I asked Mary and Chuck if they wanted to go along or wait in the cool indoors. They opted to follow us.

As we walked out of the building, I donned my sunglasses to shield my eyes from the glare off the pavement. The Gulf Stream motor home sat on the other side of the parking lot. The sides of the glossy, white exterior were gilded with maroon and ocean blue decals. The three-foot border around its skirt was a light gray. Seeing it glisten, goosebumps ran from my head to my toes.

What a package!

We no sooner arrived at the coach, when Sally began to rattle off her canned speech. In a whirlwind fashion, she proceeded around the outside of the camper. Valves, motors, and pipes cluttered my mind as I tried to remember what they were for and how to operate them. Repeatedly, I took Sally back to a compartment with a question, especially if I hadn't been able to write the answers down fast enough.

"Don't worry," Sally said as she checked another system off her list. "Everything is in the manual you'll be getting at closing."

I imagined page after page of drawings and fine print, explaining the nuts and bolts of each system. With all there was to remember, I didn't find the thought consoling, particularly with the mid-afternoon sun frying me like a hamburger on a grill. My body begged for shade, before I'd end up as a puddle, like the wicked witch of the west in the "Wizard of Oz."

The Clovers decided, after a brief encounter with the stifling heat, that they'd examine the air conditioned interior of the motor home. In the midst of Sally's narration, I glanced at my list that no longer lay flat on my clipboard. The humidity had transformed it into a moist, wrinkled piece of paper barely able to take on more ink. Regardless, at the top of my list was the water system. I had to know how to winterize the system.

In one quick motion, Sally pulled a sheet of paper from her clipboard, smiled, and handed it to me. "Read this later, it'll tell you how to winterize the unit."

"What! There's a whole list of topics attached to this I can't afford to skip over. I was told I would be shown how to do this when I bought the camper. I have to know what equipment I need, not to mention making sure the water is safe to drink. I bet the manual doesn't tell me how much chlorine to use to purify the water, does it?"

Sally hesitated. "I'm sure it must."

I pointed at the water system, "Nothing is marked, so how will I know which drains are for the main lines and which are for the fresh water tank? What about the hot water heater? How can I tell if it is full of water so I don't ruin the heating element? I'm sure there's plenty to know about protecting the pump as the temperature drops. I don't even know when to use the pump and when not to. What about the bypass and normal flow valves...?"

Sally stood staring at me with her mouth open with nothing coming out. Seeing the puzzled look on her flushed face, I paused and asked a question I hoped she could answer, "What happens if I forget to turn the pump off?"

Her facial expression brightened into a smile. She chuckled, "Oh, don't forget to turn the pump off, or it'll blow up."

"Are you serious?"

"Of course, I am. All this is really easy," came her sugary reply. "Just don't worry about it. You'll see when you read the sheet I gave you. If you still don't understand, you can always call our service department. They'll answer your questions. We have a lot more things to cover, so we'd better get busy. We're running out of time. We'll have to get you in for the closing soon."

I had been sidetracked; I gritted my teeth. I wasn't leaving the dealership without the minimum amount of instructions, no matter how late it got. I had kept Mary and Chuck waiting so long that it didn't matter.

I can't believe the pump will blow up. It might burn out, but blow up?

Referring me to other departments became Sally's diversionary tactic for unanswered questions. It was the service department: the housekeeping departments, the pre-delivery department, the maintenance department, even the RV store got in there. Obviously, Sally wasn't trained to answer a lot of questions about owning an RV. Her job consisted of reciting her canned routine, pointing out various systems.

As we continued, more and more notes were scribbled on the corners and down the sides of my lists. I wondered if I'd ever get the mess straightened out.

Seems that basic instructions have gone out of the window along with the promise to inspect the unit before closing. Learning to manage the camper will be quite a challenge. I think I'm about to become their most frequent customer.

As Sally and I entered the motor home, the Clovers were sitting on the gun-metal, blue love-seat. They were smiling like Tweety Birds after getting the best of Sylvester. I wasn't sure if I provoked their happy demeanor with my flushed, disarrayed appearance, or if it was a sign of their approval of the coach. Whatever it was, I didn't care. My body felt like it had been tossed into the throes of the Hans Selye's fight or flight syndrome as I tried to stay alive against the odds.

While Sally paused to look at her "to-do" list, I noticed that the central air had performed its duty in cooling the coach. That was one less thing to worry about.

Numerous repairs were supposed to be completed on the camper before closing. Scouting the coach, I discovered that none of them had been done: the coffee stains were still obvious on the living room carpet, the molding in the hallway had not been replaced, the bathroom door wouldn't stay closed, the vents in the floor had not been cleaned and the dead beetles were still looking down at me from the overhead vents. Remembering Mr. Snagg's attitude, fury vibrated through my body like a hot iron on a damp cloth.

These will be taken care of or I won't close. Let's see how that affects Snagg's pocketbook.

As with the exterior of the unit, Sally bounced from one thing to the next in the inside. Attempting to get organized, I asked Sally for a piece of paper. She tore a sheet from her pad and handed it to me. In between Sally's pauses, I jotted some items down that I needed to remember.

1. Service department: a.) bypass/normal valves, b.) what to do if the refrigerator doesn't go on, c.) ask about the pump blowing up.
2. Call Mark on the maintenance and service for the generator.
3. RV store: parts catalog.

My hand began to cramp. *I sure could've used some help with this. I probably should've taped it. It's a little late for that bright idea, dearie.*

"Sorry to interrupt your writing," Sally said. "But we have to get you into closing in a couple of minutes."

"Just give me a second. I don't want to forget these things."

4. Housekeeping: a.) clean the ceiling vents, b.) stains out of the carpet, c.) clean the floor vents.
5. Pre-delivery: a.) fix bathroom door, b.) broken floor vent, c.) re-install the hallway molding.
6. Closing agent: a.) inverter, b.) carpet stains.

As soon as I looked up, Sally began her pitiless routine. How could she possibly know what it was like to be more than forty, fifty, or sixty? I had been seized by exhaustion. My head hummed. Stomach cramps joined the one key melodious buzz at regular intervals. I used the little energy I had left to tell Sally about the items that I wanted completed while I was in closing. Then I stood in silence as she continued to point. My listening ability had turned inward to join the hum in my head. Not one more piece of information would be absorbed.

Chapter 10

Sally continued to chatter as we walked back to the waiting room, "It will only be about fifteen minutes before closing. As soon as you're finished come back to the coach."

Mary and Chuck were sitting in the waiting room with magazines in hand. As I looked at them, I thanked the Lord such gracious people offered to help with the transportation. I dropped myself into one of the hard chairs next to Mary, bowed my head, and closed my eyes. Just maybe there'd be enough time to recover my brain before the next attack.

Jolted by the mention of my name, I realized I had dozed off.

Mary shook me gently. "It's time to buy that motor home," she said, in a sing-song tune.

A man in his twenties, more round than tall, with coal black hair, stood before me. "I'm Bill. I'll be handling the closing for you. Would you please follow me?"

My eyes burned as I looked up at him. I wasn't sure I'd be able to read anything, much less understand it. With the personality of a corpse, he turned and walked toward the hallway. I lifted a body that felt like concrete out of the chair. The next challenge would be to keep up. However, my best effort put me many steps behind Bill as I began my pursuit. Unable to maintain pace, I decided he could continue on his journey without me. If I didn't arrive at whatever destination, he'd come looking for me. Ha! That didn't happen. He was standing outside his office by the time I guessed my way through the maze. As I approached, Mr. Personality pointed to where I should sit. A manual at least four inches thick sat in front of my place. Thoughts of small print and multiple drawings returned to permeate my brain. My insides groaned. Bill pushed the manual aside, clearing the table for the stack of closing documents.

Before he started, I wanted to make sure we were on the same page. We weren't. The glitch had to do with the inverter and the coffee stains. Bill insisted I had misunderstood about the inverter. I was supposed to get a converter, not an inverter.

I argued.

He repeated himself.

I got ticked. A frazzled mind and an exhausted body had a tendency to make me rather testy.

Picking up my purse, I whipped out the advertisement I had received by e-mail before I had bought the coach.

Jaw clenched, I pointed at the word in the ad and spelled *i-n- v- e- r- t- e- r*.

He glared at me.

I stared him down. I wanted what was mine. His jowl dropped; his eyes widened. Defeat was written on his face.

See Appendix 3: Advertisement for inverter.

I had no idea how much one cost, but I did know it allowed me to draw electricity off the chassis batteries for dry camping. Plugged into the port on the dashboard, the computer and television would run for about five to six hours. I'd be too chicken to attempt it for that long.

Bill changed the subject so I assumed he thought he would win the next round. He reminded me that the dealership couldn't be responsible for the stains in the carpet as I bought a used unit.

Try again, fellow, because that won't work! These were the things I had been promised and I want them one way or another.

Growling on the inside and smiling on the outside, I calmly told him I wouldn't close without the inverter or without the carpet being cleaned.

A brilliant display of pink, from collar to the crown of his black hair, revealed his position. Acting nonchalant, as though his lovely color didn't show, he picked up the phone and dialed a number.

"I need some assistance over here."

Before you could snap your fingers, the sales manager walked into Bill's office and asked him to leave. When the manager saw the advertisement, he left the room.

I felt like a hundred guppies were swimming through my stomach as I waited to see what he'd do about the inverter.

Ten minutes later the sales manager returned, "I don't know what happened to the one that was in the motor home. The staff couldn't find it so I brought you a new one."

Thrilled, I thanked him. The company would pay to clean and dye the carpet, if necessary. As diplomatically as I could, I mentioned the earlier delays. I told him I hadn't received the instructions that I had been promised. Without hesitation he gave me permission to bring the motor home back on my way to Florida. My stress level dropped from a ten to a three.

A lot of frustration could've been avoided if he'd been around a few hours ago.

Feeling he had been fair, I shifted my attitude to pleasant, but guarded.

The sun was just above the horizon when I finished signing the papers. After closing, I walked to the coach, like the nursery rhyme—"dragging my tail behind me." Thanks to the sales manager, my final list for Sally had shrunk a great deal. However, I still hoped to have some things taken care of before I left.

1. The pre-delivery list that was given Mr. Jack Snagg.

See Appendix 4: Pre-Delivery Instructions-Used.

2. Check fluid levels in the motor and air pressure for the tires.
3. Awning: raising and lowering it, plus maintenance.
4. Hydraulic jacks: leveling the coach, plus maintenance.

The jacks were the most important. I'd be using them every day, especially if I dry camped in places like WalMart or Flying J's.

Although I have a good sense of balance, walking on a slope would soon convert my golf putter into a cane to support my lower back. The shaft was already bent from its master's demands.

I could see Sally standing next to the unit as I walked out of the door. Miss Congeniality immediately congratulated me on my purchase. The glow of ownership made butterflies airborne in my stomach. I looked at the motor home with a dazed smile and handed my list to Sally.

Let her tackle the items as she wishes. I'm too tired for any more confusion. It's just not worth it.

But Sally had a different idea. She began to take the awning down. With what little energy I had left, I flipped through the manual looking for the "How To's."

"Don't bother," Sally said. "There's nothing in there on the awning. You'll just have to pay close attention. It's pretty easy."

She's got to be kidding!

I tried. Oh, how I tried, but my brain would not compute. The awning went down and back up again so fast I hardly knew it happened. The only thing I remembered was I should never let go of the cord. If I did, the awning would go up, entwining the cord inside. Fear recorded this piece of information, fast! The awning had gained a spot on my list for the return trip to the dealer in November.

Sally ignored the question on the tire pressure. As it was a no-brainer compared to the rest, I let it pass.

The hydraulic jacks were the next thing to come under attack. Sally proceeded to push the arrows on the control panel by the driver's seat, going back and forth between the top, the bottom, and the side arrows. I tried to squeeze between her

40

and the cab door to see what she was doing, but I failed the squeeze. All I could see were two arrows on the top section, two on the bottom, and two on either side.

As Sally began to work with the jacks, she gushed out a jet-propelled lesson. "To make the jacks come down, you'll need to push the arrows that are pointing up. To make the jacks go up, you'll have to push the arrows that are pointing down. The same is true with the arrows on either side. With the red ones on, just keep pushing the up or the down arrow on the side until the yellow light comes on and the red one goes out. When the coach is level, the yellow lights should be on and the red ones should be out. Whatever you do, don't ever leave two red lights on at the same time. One is OK, but never two."

Why? I had no idea. Either I'd ask someone with a motor home, call the company or put it on the November list. It ended up on the same page with the pump blowing up and never letting go of the awning cord.

Being unsuccessful at leveling the coach, one that was sitting on an almost level lot, Sally said, "Oh, you'll just have to play around with the arrows until you get the hang of it."

Unwilling to accept her comment, I asked for help from the service department. Either the heat of the day or the tone of my voice made her decide not to give me an argument. She dialed a number on her cell phone and requested that a technician come to the coach. I had to have somebody with some knowhow explain this procedure. It couldn't be that complicated. I wished the Clovers were listening, but they had set up their own routine long ago, browsing the RV store, reading in the waiting room or straightening the inside of their car.

The technician arrived within a couple of minutes, greeted me, and began fiddling with the arrows on the control panel, making the coach jump around in a little dance. To my dismay, he didn't appear to have any more expertise than Sally.

After several attempts to level the coach, he said, "The jacks are coming down fine, ma'am. You'll get the hang of it."

I tried to tell him it wasn't a question of whether or not they came down. I wanted to know if they would level the coach. Unfortunately, I was as unsuccessful at getting my point across as he was at leveling the coach. I voiced other concerns that the technician couldn't solve, like checking the transmission fluid for the jacks. My attitude had taken a back-slide down past "guarded."

I began to wonder if each department had a job description that read, "If you aren't sure, send the problem to another department." In the meantime, the unlucky customer wondered why he decided to buy a motor home.

It had been a long day and we still had to drive home. I never should've mentioned the final list. Very few of the items were done. All it did was keep us from leaving sooner. Knowing I could bring the coach back in November, I held further words.

Chapter 11

Blackness filled the parking lot as the lights from the RV store went out, one by one. Ownership had put me behind the wheel of this big rig for the next 180 miles. I'd be traveling through numerous small towns on a very dark night. My only driving experience with a camper had been limited to going around the block at the time of contract. Hart City had given me more training than Mr. Snagg. It didn't matter how far I had driven, it was still the first time on my own and at night. I didn't have the luxury of being a chicken.

When I pulled myself into the seat, comfort enveloped me as I sank into the cushioned leather. Two sets of keys overflowed in my hand. Putting one set in my pocket, I began looking for the one for the ignition. The big 450-V10 roared to a start as soon as I turned the key. I felt a surge of excitement in my weary body. I positioned the seat and pulled the knob to turn on the headlights. The clock on the wood-trimmed dashboard flashed 9:30. Habit took my hand to the rear view mirror. Then it dropped. Unless I raised the back blind, I'd only be able to see the interior of the coach. I adjusted the side mirrors to include a safe portion of the road and the motor home. Then I took a quick mental inventory.

I sure can't afford to forget anything. Let's see, the jacks are up, the antenna is down, the step is in, and the bathroom door is closed, for now anyway. I'm sure it will be flapping open a few times since it hasn't been fixed.

Sighing, I settled back to begin my journey. I released the emergency and shifted into drive. The smooth motion of the camper created the feeling of floating on a cloud. With great respect for its size, versus my size, I slowly applied pressure to the gas pedal. The rig responded and gained momentum. The vehicle moved out of the lot and onto the road behind the Clovers. Mary set the pace with her little Honda. I tried to keep up—much like an elephant following a mouse.

Before long the dial on the speedometer reached forty-five miles an hour. For some reason, forty-five seemed a lot faster then the fifty-five Mary drove on the way down.

Having traveled the road a couple of times, I knew the highway would narrow in another mile. My heart raced and my grip tightened on the steering wheel with the thought of on-coming traffic. Dew hung low, like mist over the sea. Ever so often headlights from an approaching car broke through the haze, giving the blacktop a slippery appearance. I released the gas pedal to compensate for the effect. My speed dropped five to ten miles an hour. Darkness swallowed the road, before and behind me. Every bump in the road jarred my heart into skipping a beat.

Trying to keep the wide-body camper between the white line on my right and the yellow on my left became a balancing act.

The Clovers' tail-lights had gotten miniscule. The slippery appearance of the road created an illusion of the coach slipping into the deep gulley alongside the road. I forced myself to focus on the lines and not on the lack of a shoulder. Regardless, I hung on to the steering wheel as though it could save me from disaster.

I have a long drive ahead of me. Dwelling on a catastrophe won't prevent one, but sure could cause one. I have to think about something else.

My choices were praying, singing, or deep breathing. The prayer took priority. I should've done that before my foot hit the gas pedal.

Here I am again, Father, scaring myself to death. If I'd just remember to ask for Your help before I panicked, I'd sure save myself a lot of grief. Please forgive me for being late as usual and send me some help, fast. That is, if it be Your will. And by the way, an angel to nudge me if I start falling asleep would be nice. In Jesus' name, I thank You, Father!

Now that I had put my immediate future in God's hands, I could get my mind on something more relaxing. I didn't have enough energy to sing, so I chose the deep breathing. After five minutes of a concerted effort to release my grip on the steering wheel, I began to relax.

By the time I reached highway 3, a double lane highway around Muncie, Indiana, I had caught up to Mary and Chuck. Noticing that visibility was getting worse, I decided we needed a break. The parking lot at McDonald's in Warsaw would work. It had plenty of room for the RV.

Business lights—some on and some off—on either side of the street accented the glare on the road. Finding the MacDonald's under these conditions could get tricky. I slowed my speed, watching for their sign. I put on my directional to signal Mary for a stop. She pulled into the lot right behind me.

Mary and Chuck crawled out of the car. It was obvious that the heat of the day and the energy required to be patient had taken its toll. sadly, MacDonald's was closed; only the security lights glowed in the dark. Our needs would have to wait.

I slid out of the driver's seat, stiff and aching. Together we hobbled around the empty lot, conversing about the hunger pains and the need for a potty break.

As the Clovers lived north of Warsaw, we agreed to head our separate ways. They were more than willing to see me home, but with the poor visibility and the lateness of the hour, safety had to be the first consideration. They had given me the gift of time, never complaining. I thanked God for the blessing of their company as I turned west onto highway 30 and they continued north.

I arrived home at one fifteen in the morning. I pulled the unit to a stop on Lowell Street, a half a block from my house. At such a late hour I wasn't up to dealing with all those arrows to level the coach on my street. As I parked the camper, the streetlight cast shadows into the darkness, blurring my vision and blackening the curb. Lacking experience with parking a big rig, I had to get out of my new home several times to check my position. My front stuck out in the road and my backend hugged the curb. Back and forth I went with this scene until the back wheels were not touching the curb and the front wheels were a little closer. It would have to be good enough—I needed a bathroom.

Reaching to the dash, I turned on the interior lights and picked up my purse. Somewhere in the mess of the day was a house key. I searched one pocket after another. Not finding one, I dumped its contents onto the passenger's seat. My bladder told me I'd better hurry. Then it dawned on me. I hadn't driven. My house keys were on the key chain in the house with the car keys. The garage door opener was in the car that was parked inside the garage.

Now what am I going to do? I don't think it's safe to sleep in the camper. Besides, I don't know the city code. Be just my luck to have an officer banging on my door at three in the morning. There's no water anyway, so I can't use the bathroom.

My eighty-year-old neighbors, who lived behind me, had a key. I didn't want to disturb them, or worse, frighten them at such a late hour. Urgency convinced me they were often up half the night anyway.

With a mild case of guilt I rang their doorbell. Scotty, a spry, elderly gentleman came to the door. Dressed in his bathrobe with white hair tousled, he asked how the trip went. Trying not to think about the unnerving, tingling pain in my lower abdomen, I gave him a brief description. I owed him that much for his kindness.

He chuckled when I told him I was locked out. "OK, I suppose you'd like to have your key?"

I thanked him and his wife and promised I'd be over in the afternoon to fill them in on all the details.

As I turned the key in my front door, I had a revelation. I could've used the bathroom in the unit, even without water. A little tinkle in the toilet, what could it hurt? Waking my neighbors and letting Mary and Chuck suffer showed I wasn't using much sense. But after the day we had, making it home safely would've been considered a miracle in itself.

Before my head hit the pillow, I paused and said, *"Thank you, God, for a safe trip for all of us. Thank you for gracious neighbors and for the gift of the motor home. Especially bless Mary and Chuck for the love and support they gave me this day. I ask it in Jesus' precious name. You know. . . I'm one lucky duck.*

Chapter 12

The sun peeked through the thin metal strips of the forest-green mini-blind, forcing me to consciousness. Little by little my mind became aware of belonging to a body that had been abused beyond belief. Squinting, I lifted my head just enough to see the time. The clock with its large green digital numerals displayed eight forty-five. I moaned as my head dropped back into the pillow. I didn't want to move. However, my mind didn't care about my aching body. The chores that were outlined on a piece of paper in the kitchen were living in my brain.

Although soft and huggable, my pillow wouldn't get the chores done or still my brain from its narration.

I think the minor surgery on my left arm is next Wednesday. Before that I have to get everything ready for the trip to Wisconsin.

"Seems like every time I turn around the medical profession is after my body. Must have hit some kind of a magical time with my age."

You'd think I'd learn that a doctor sees a nurse who's fighting his diagnoses, like a mouse trying to swim up Niagara Falls.

I kept telling him I hurt it when I lifted my bike; of course, he focused on the test results, not on my self-diagnosis. Then he hit me with the MRI and said it could be a malignant tumor, like a sarcoma.

When my opinion became redundant, he got my attention by saying, Whatever it is, it hasn't attached to the bone...yet.

The finale came when he switched gears and said the surgery wasn't a big deal.

"Well it was to me."

Soon I'll have to call Minnesota to make plans to visit with my brother. I suppose the motor home should be washed and waxed. Ugh! Hope it's not as bad as the fifth wheel. After I come back from Wisconsin I'll worry about arrangements for my fiftieth class reunion, and making a reservation at a campground in Florida. Oh! I can't forget about Richmond for the motor home repairs.

"I might call David's sister-in-law Nickie in Venice, Florida. Maybe she'd like to get together for a short visit and I can show off my new toy. Doesn't hurt to know somebody in the area where I plan to stay. I can't believe the doctor said I'd be able to drive and lift things. Doesn't a wound need time to heal?"

My Cuddle Ewe, an all wool pad, lay beneath the mattress cover. It kept me cool in the summer and toasty warm in the winter. I squirmed a little and nestled into its softness. I wanted to stay there forever. Of course that wouldn't work. I stretched long and hard, saying good morning to my Maker as I gave into my list of chores.

Hoping I had worked some of the knots out of my body, I grabbed the side of the mattress and pulled myself into a sitting position. Doing so, my foot arched into a charlie horse. I jumped out of bed and began hobbling around, through the living room, through the dining room, through the kitchen, in an effort to walk it out. Eternity came and went before I finally won the battle. If that was intended to be my jumpstart for the day, it worked.

Poking my head into the refrigerator, I decided a good breakfast would keep the hunger pangs at bay until suppertime. The day had begun without me, and I'd have to play catch-up.

The pending surgery had me concerned. I never believed the MRI. However, the surgery was performed and more involved than predicted. The location of the resection, a highly innervated area, caused burning. Pain medication made me sick and trying to ignore it wasn't working. The doctor didn't hold any positive expectations for recovery for the nerve pain within the near future. Somehow, I'd have to get the pain under control. I needed to get to Wisconsin for my RV training session before my son left for elk hunting in September, and it was already August.

With a concerted effort, I tried different things. Ice helped for a little while, but I couldn't drive 300 miles with one arm packed in ice. The next attempt succeeded. I wrapped an ace bandage around my hand all the way to my elbow. Having the area covered decreased the intensity of the pain, making it bearable.

The final diagnosis was an arterial venial malfunction, which translated to—I hurt it when I lifted my bike.

Guess the mouse made it to the top of Niagara falls after all.

Chapter 13

Greg, my youngest son, said he would teach me about living in an RV on his family's thirty-seven acres. He had put an extra clean out on his septic when he and his wife, Teresa, built their home. This would provide my training session with full hook-ups, water, electric and sewer.

After leaving Greg's I'd go to Minnesota to see my brother Bob. He was losing his battle against colon cancer. After that I'd drive back to Indiana to get ready to go to Milwaukee for my fiftieth class reunion. I loved the idea of showing up in a motor home, especially at my age. I'd certainly be a novelty item. My angel reminded me, with a gentle nudge, that it was a gift. I needed to deflate my airborne ego and get back on track.

The repairs in Richmond would be the easiest to arrange as the tech said I only had to give a week's notice for an appointment.

I tried to make sense out of the RV manual as I rested the first week after surgery. Page after page of technical information caused my brain to yawn and my eyes to glaze into a blank stare.

The previous owner had organized the manual into what he thought most important. The satellite dish held first place. In mine the satellite dish would be at the end and the refrigerator would be in the front. After an experience with David in Quartzite, Arizona, I didn't need a reminder that the RV's refrigerator had to be leveled and cooled for 24 hours before placing food in it. The "p's and q's" for a refrigerator had to be followed, period.

One of the technicians at the dealership assured me that they weren't as touchy as they used to be as long as the refrigerator, not the coach, was close to being level. I believed that like I believed elephants can fly. I had no intentions of taking any chances, especially after finding out they cost megabucks to replace.

Quartzite, Arizona, was a desert town where all life meets at its four corners. As soon as David noticed that our refrigerator had malfunctioned, he paged through the manual. We didn't have any time to waste. The temperature had climbed to the nineties, even though it was January. Looking through the manual David managed to find a Wilderness repair shop right in town. As David drove the coach through the company's gates, a pleasingly plump man approached.

"We're about to close, folks," the man said.

David explained our predicament and, as agreeable as a person could be, he said, "You can park inside the gates until I have time to take a look in the morning. There's a plug over on the side of the building so you'll have electric. I have a couple of bags of ice in my deep freeze. We'll throw them in your refrigerator. This will keep things cold for you. By the way, my name is Jake. Have a pleasant evening, folks."

Early the next morning Jake knocked on our door, "I'd like to take a look at the refrigerator before the day gets too crazy."

"Sure. Come on in," David said.

53

I curled up on the dinette to watch the action. Jake began pushing buttons on the control panel at the top of the refrigerator—no response.

In a calm manner, Jake said, "It looks like we'll either have to replace the control panel or burp the refrigerator, sir. Of course, if the burping doesn't work, I'll still have to put in a new refrigerator. It's your choice."

We looked at each other with eyes that said, "Huh."

Jake politely accommodated our ignorance by explaining the burping process.

"This is how it's done, folks. The fellows will take the trim off from around the refrigerator and then gradually ease it out of its space. Once it's out we'll take it into the plant and turn it upside down. After about twenty-four hours I'll know if the Freon is flowing again. If it is, you'll be OK. If not, I'm afraid you'll need a new refrigerator."

The cost for this burping in 1994 was a mere five hundred dollars. However, a new refrigerator would be twelve hundred. We went for the burping and hoped we wouldn't have to buy a refrigerator on top of the burping.

Under Jake's direction, the workmen gently pried the refrigerator from its housing. Reluctantly, the refrigerator yielded under the pressure. As it did, it dropped some not such welcomed travelers off its sides. One and a half to three inch long box-elder bugs were clinging to it for all they were worth. I withdrew my legs, faster than you could say Peter Piper, and I scrunched into the corner of the dinette. As they dropped to the floor, they crept in all directions. I hurled my arms around my body with a strangle hold while I watched their antennas wheel in a circular motion in hopes of being reunited with their safe environment. My skin crawled and headed in the opposite direction.

Looking straight ahead into the gaping hole, I saw that there were another thousand buried in the insulation. Frozen in horror, I stood on the seat of the dinette with my back flat against the wall. Their appearance was my signal to make a disappearance. I screamed my retreat.

Later that day, the workman chuckled as he assured me there weren't any more bugs in the coach. Somewhat relieved, yet not entirely certain, I tried to put the bugs out of my mind. After all, we were camping and bugs go with camping, don't they?

The next morning, while doing my hair, my attention was drawn to an object behind me in the mirror.

A giant box-elder bug was doing a tightrope act on the cord of my curling iron.

Terrified, I listened to myself scream as I pitched the iron to its death.

David rushed to save the bug.

"It's only a bug. It's not going to hurt you. They're harmless."

"Nothing that big is harmless," I snapped.

Thankfully, the refrigerator burped like a baby. So we didn't have to buy a new one. I decided, right then and there, if I ever found myself surrounded by crawling creatures that had captured my motor home, I'd sell it or burn it.

55

*　　*　　*

Loading the camper after the surgery would be a big job, with only one good arm. I taught transfer techniques in nursing, but they weren't as impressive as David's.

Right after his disease caused him to lose his ability to speak, our dishwasher began to leak. Wouldn't you know, he insisted on going to Circuit City. He had been watching the ads and they had the best buys. I begged him to reconsider. I could live without a dishwasher for awhile, but he said "no." He intended to stick to his agenda.

Arriving at Circuit City, David found enough energy to look at every dishwasher on the display floor. By this time, David had to do his communicating with pencil and paper.

Seeing us, a salesman approached. David presented his "want list" as he began to negotiate the prices on his pad. The salesman's face flushed as he argued with a man who couldn't speak. After arriving at a sales price on a Kitchen Aid, David wrote, "Put it in the trunk."

Einstein would've gasped.

The size of the trunk of our 1990 Dodge Spirit just couldn't make the cut.

"It'll never fit!" I shouted.

This didn't faze anybody. Three men stretched the opening of the trunk beyond reason to accommodate the appliance and crisscrossed nylon rope over its back to secure the huge box that left two-thirds of the dishwasher hanging precariously outside of the trunk. It looked like a giant fish that grabbed some bait it couldn't quite grasp.

I declared my next jewel of wisdom, "We'll never make it home."

David grinned and nodded, "yes," as he got into the passenger seat.

On the way I continued to check the rear view mirror, sure that the dishwasher would end up in somebody's lap.

Feeling trapped by what I felt was an unsafe situation, my arms trembled as I hung on to the steering wheel. I hadn't thought about how we'd get it into the house. First I'd have to get it to the house.

As soon as we arrived home, David began untying the ropes. I begged him to wait until I could get a neighbor to help.

He shook his head.

Using leverage, he rolled the box out of the trunk. I rushed to help him as I mumbled complaints of insanity under my breath.

Back and forth, side to side, we scooted the heavy box on the concrete that grabbed the cardboard tighter with every inch gained. When we reached the front step, David rolled the box onto the stoop. The last roll put it into the house.

David sat down in his recliner to catch his breath and to mull over a plan. In the meantime, I tugged; I pushed and pulled on the box, hoping I could get it into the kitchen. I couldn't budge it.

A playful smile crossed his face as he watched me struggle. Then he sat down on the floor, planted both feet against the bottom of the carton and extended his legs. Like an inchworm, he slid the dishwasher into the kitchen.

Looking at the camper I had to laugh about his ingenuity. I'd follow his leverage examples and get the job done.

Chapter 14

As I made repeated trips to the motor home to load it, the neighbors became more and more intrigued. One after another showed up for some show and tell time; however, no one offered to help. After five days of pacing myself, the coach was ready to roll.

I asked Paul, my neighbor at the end of the block, if I could plug the coach into his outside receptacle. My street was sloped, whereas his was level. This would reduce the possibility of having to burp the refrigerator.

"Sure," Paul said.

Everything was going as fine as eating s'mores over a campfire. After I parked the unit alongside of Paul's home, I plugged it into his receptacle. Then I went inside with a spring to my step.

Upon reaching the refrigerator, my spring sprung. The refrigerator had not switched from gas to electric. Instead, my nervous system shifted to, "Oh no, now what?"

Come on, get a grip! You're not even on the road yet. How do you think you'll ever handle problems then if you can't handle them now?

Then it dawned on me. Maybe Paul's outlet was bad. He tested the plug with a small radio and found that it was. After tripping his breakers, the radio went on. Thinking I had solved the problem, and acting smugly smart, I hopped back into the camper. The refrigerator had not responded.

I called the dealership. The technician asked if I had used the adapter for the house. Of course, I had. Then he told me how to take the back off the refrigerator to see if it was plugged in. After spending ten minutes finding the right screwdriver and taking the plate off, I realized the refrigerator wouldn't have blown my neighbor's outlet if it hadn't been plugged in. Oh well, now I knew how to take the back off of the refrigerator.

"You'll have to bring the camper back to Richmond so we can see what's wrong," he said.

"I'm not doing that."

Dah!

"Somehow, I'll figure it out."

After two hours of plugging and unplugging, moving the coach, and blowing out each electrical service as I went from neighbor to neighbor, David's past words surfaced.

"Don't ever plug the electric for the fifth wheel into any socket except the one in the middle of the garage."

Between his guru status as a master electrician and the incident with the truck mirrors, I didn't ask why. After my brain power kick in, I figured the center outlet must have had more amps. I found a neighbor who knew he had at least twenty amps, plugged in the coach, and the little light on the refrigerator lit up nice and bright. Needless to say, life would've been a lot simpler if I hadn't had this memory lapse.

"When are you planning to leave?" Paul asked when I saw him the next day.

"Early tomorrow morning, regardless of the weather. My youngest son is waiting to give me a crash course on living in an RV. He lives in northern Wisconsin; and he's scheduled to leave for elk hunting. I don't have much time to learn a lot."

"Remember, if you don't know how to fix something, just ask. None of us knows how to do everything. Besides, there's always someone who is willing to help. First and foremost is to be safe."

"Thanks for the advice. I'll see you this fall."

See Appendix 8: Motor Home: Items to Take.

Before I walked to the house, I checked my list for loading the motor home. I hadn't missed anything. I planned to leave for Wisconsin at five in the morning. As I crawled into bed, I pondered the adventure. The Cuddle Ewe comforted my body as I mulled over the trip, until a sinking feeling crept into the pit of my stomach. As I became more nauseous, I realized David always got sick before a trip. Other than saying he didn't feel good, he never said what could be bothering him. He'd just hurry to the bathroom in a stoop position, making sure I saw him.

If I remember correctly, his symptoms didn't begin until after we sold the twenty-six foot rig and bought the thirty- eight foot fifth wheel. This never made sense to me. He wanted the bigger unit, not me. I was content with the smaller one; it was cute, comfortable, and affordable. David didn't agree. He didn't want to spend five or six months out of the year, sitting in a little twenty-six foot fifth wheel. I wondered how long I'd lay in bed contemplating my queasiness before I'd get up to do something about it. Of course, I felt sure that I'd start feeling better any second. Fifteen minutes went by and then thirty. By the time I rolled out of bed, I knew why David got sick. A lot of responsibility sat at the end of the block. A big motor home with all of its own secrets. One thing for sure, before I tackled that rig, I needed to have a good night's sleep. Warm milk here I come.

The sun had already started the day as I closed the garage door. The morning air fell still, fresh. I would be blessed with another beautiful sunrise, walking toward the coach.

Every time I see a sunrise, I'm reminded of one of my elderly patients. One morning I found her staring out of her fourth floor hospital window as I made my nursing rounds. Walking around to her side to see what had captured her gaze, I stood in silence. Vibrant shades of fuchsia melted over the light, gray clouds that hid hints of the baby blue sky. I watched, spellbound.

After this display of glory broke into the new day, she turned to me and said, "God has such a beautiful way of saying good morning, doesn't He?"

I placed my arm around her shoulder and gave her a gentle hug. Her words were forever etched in my heart. I gazed at the coach, another blessing. I whispered. "Thanks again, Father, for this incredible gift."

I went through the outside checklist before entering the coach.

Lock the bins, put the electric step in, make sure the television antenna is down and the awning locked.

Completing the outside checks, I unlocked the door and pulled myself into the driver's seat. My stomach was still s little upset. As I turned the key in the ignition, the 450-V10 roared to a start. My stomach settled down as my body responded with the same type of tingles I had the first time I started it.

I set the emergency brake, leaving the motor running while I checked off the items on my inside list. This was overkill as no one had been inside; however, my common sense reminded me that I needed to start a routine to avoid the beginning of carelessness. An accident could soon become its companion.

As I walked through the coach, I saw that the refrigerator had switched from electric to gas automatically and the pump was off, so far so good. My steps felt light as I finished the inspection. It was a grand feeling, like standing tall. A sense of freedom had been born, a vision of independence. The future held peaceful moments that would shut out the world of violence and confusion.

See Appendix 5 and 6 for the Inside and Outside check list. Taken from "Highways" magazine put out by the Good Sam's club.

Chapter 15

As I headed toward Chicago, dishes, cookie sheets and silverware clattered with every pothole. Going around Chicago for the first time with the motor home would be a nerve-racking experience, without everything rattling in the background. Even my hearing aids, programmed to cut out noise, were bent on magnifying it. No doubt I would have to do a better job to silence them or not complain about the concert. All I could do at this point was ignore the performance.

In spite of the traffic, I made it around Chicago with minimal grief. What more could I ask? Hold on—there's more. Around the Racine area my left side-view mirror decided to make a trip of its own. Slowly, it worked its way toward the driver's door, making it impossible to see passing traffic. I had to attend to this before I ended up greeting somebody the wrong way. First I'd have to find a place to stop so I could correct the situation. Didn't plan to adjust anything on the Interstate.

At the next exit my eyes scanned the countryside for an area large enough for the camper, definitely paranoid. Leaving the motor running, I set the emergency brake, got out of the RV, and pushed the arm on the mirror.

It didn't budge.

With a little logic, I decided that if pushing doesn't work, try pulling. After a little muscle and a lot of determination, it moved to where it was at the beginning of the trip. I couldn't see any screws to tighten so I hoped that it would stay put.

The next 120 miles to Greg and Teresa's became an unplanned ritual, stop—adjust—go— stop—adjust—go. Every movement of the mirror added frustration, not to mention a considerable amount of time to the trip.

Common sense and the law prompted me to keep the fifty-five miles an hour speed limit, a snail's pace for someone who drove seventy to seventy-five. However, I didn't have a clue as to how long it would take to stop the camper at any speed.

For the first time in my life, I wasn't the one doing the passing. Little cars zigzagged around other little cars in a whistle. I thought the monstrous trucks that lumbered down the road would've slowed their maneuvers. On the contrary, nothing kept them from acting like they were on an obstacle course and certainly indestructible.

With lines of traffic visible for miles in the distance, I wondered what they thought they could accomplish, other than a quick death. I exclaimed a few unmentionable adjectives in the process of their zigging and zagging. Did they leave a margin for error? Not that I could see. As traffic began to pick up speed, a small space opened in front of my coach. I had been granted a safety net, a breather. Seconds later, a small car slid in front of me.

The traffic slowed. *She slammed on her brakes.*

Panic burned my body as my foot went for the brakes. I had over fifteen thousand pounds to stop in a mini-second.

Fear didn't have time to register its awareness as I watched the front of the coach speed toward the back of her car. With all my strength I pushed on the brakes, pumping them for more traction.

My eyes shifted in fractions of a second to my side-view mirrors and back to the impending crisis. The camper responded much quicker than I anticipated. Nevertheless, by the time I released the breath I had been holding, the motor home was within a foot of her back bumper.

A split second later, I screamed out of my window, "Are you crazy? You're lucky I didn't squash you like a bug!"

She ignored my scream.

I grumbled, "It's a good thing everybody doesn't drive like she does."

Undoubtedly, this is how road rage began because I wanted to strangle her for the jolt she gave to my nervous system.

This was not the best way to find out how fast the motor home could stop. Now if I could just slow my heart rate that quick.

The journey neared its end as I reached Black Creek, Wisconsin. I had about twelve miles to go to Greg and Teresa's. My beacon would be a little tan shed, outhouse size, which sat on the corner of the family's acreage. It was a place for my three granddaughters to wait for the school bus on cold winter mornings. For the life of me I couldn't imagine those three girls in such a small space without killing each other.

I finally spotted the shed. Thrilled that I had found the driveway, I turned on my directional. The dirt road looked narrower than I remembered: my tummy tingled with uncertainty.

Just take it slow and easy. There's plenty of room. You won't fall into the ditch. Your imagination is working overtime again.

I took a deep breath and made the turn. The brush along the gulley on either side of the road reached out its tentacles to claw at the coach. Attempting to soothe my overzealous imagination, I checked to make sure the backend cleared the shed. It stayed put so I assumed I missed it. All I had to do was aim the coach down the middle of the narrow gravel drive. I rode the rock-a-bye motion on the uneven surface like an old mare heading for the barn. Then I spotted my three granddaughters. They were waiting as Grandma drove up in her new rig. I was headed for hugs and kisses.

After the greetings, I got the impression I was the second reason for the excited embraces. They all had their eyes fixed on the coach. Giggles filled the air as the girls waited for me to unlock the side door. I pushed the button for the electric step and when it slid out—a sigh of approval echoed in the warmth of the afternoon. Entering one at a time, they each found what they considered the best seat in the house. Then they jumped up to explore the rest of the coach. The hit of the day was a brief ride on the sofa as the slide glided outward. Awed, the girls would be my guests for at least the next few days.

Greg, a trim thirty-seven year old with a receding hair line and a devilish laugh, rotated between days and nights on his job. My training would be sandwiched between his work schedule. When he was able, he completed a repair or two on the RV, like fixing the bathroom door so it stayed closed, replacing the molding on the ceiling, and making a longer hose into a shorter version for my black water sprayer. In the end, I got a lesson and, for sure, a test on what he did.

Of course one of my biggest concerns was emptying the black water. I had watched David many times, but as I said, seeing and doing are two different things.

The first day Greg and I worked together, he showed me how to empty and flush the tanks. As I had been living in the motor home during my training period, the tank would be full and needed to be emptied. It had been a used unit, so I couldn't be sure the indicator lights were accurate. A history lesson from my fifth wheel days taught me it wasn't smart to push your luck in the black water department. There were tons of horror stories about sewage spilling into the coach on the way to a dump site. . . no thank you. My stomach would never be up to that scenario.

It was a perfect day to tackle this not so nice job—sunny, but not too hot. Before I got into the motor home I hollered to Greg, "Let's do it."

"Ok," he shouted.

I could see Greg in my side-view mirrors as he guided me back toward the clean out for the septic. He knew more about this backing up routine than I did because he stood right where he could be seen. David had put me in charge of guiding him into a campsite one time. I didn't have the faintest idea what to do. He insisted anyway.

"It's an easy task," he said. "All you have to do is make sure I don't hit anything."

I figured I could handle that, until he couldn't see me in the side-view mirror. His mistake became mine as he bellowed, "If you can't see me, then I can't see you, either. So you tell me, how am I supposed to know which way you want me to turn?"

Being a lady, I considered that to be a rhetorical question, but my mind spoke a sentence or two in response.

I got the coach into position over the clean out with Greg's help. Proud of myself, I jumped out of the cab, awaiting a pat on the back for a good job. He had a look on his face that said, "This is normal stuff, Mom."

He stood with his arms crossed, leaning against the coach. It didn't look like he planned to move around much. My stance took on the same look as I waited for him to empty the tanks.

"What are you waiting for?" he asked.

"Aren't you going to hook up the hoses?" I whined.

Grinning from ear to ear, he said, "Oh no you don't. This is your baby. You aren't going to get a better testing ground than right here. You won't have anybody helping you on the road so it's best you make your mistakes with me watching."

"But I'm your mother," I implored to no avail.

He chuckled and pointed to the job, "Better get busy."

I put on my rubber gloves, hauled out the sewer hose, and attempted to unscrew the cap from the black water valve. Being unsuccessful, I grabbed the hammer and began banging on the little tab that protruded from its side.

"Oh no!" Greg shouted. "Don't hit that little tab. If you can't get the cap off, tap on it, don't bang on it. A little Vaseline will help it turn easier. Look here! You can hit the part that encircles the notch around the cap, but go easy on it."

The next five minutes were spent fumbling with the sewer hose that refused to be attached to the valve. In the secrecy of my mind, I wondered if I'd be able to unscrew the lid to his clean out. Wouldn't it be a bummer to get everything set up and not be able to get the sewer open? I made a mental note to unscrew the sewer cap first, before proceeding.

As it was, I've never been very good at screwing things on and off. Somehow, I manage to go right when I should go left, tightening a screw beyond belief. My daughter told me, "Remember this, Mom, *right—on!*" She also came up with a "hidey-didey" rhyme which was more complicated than trying to remember which way to turn the nozzle. Well, I'm here to tell you the *"right on"* suggestion doesn't always work, either. On a motor home connection can be doubled, back to back. That changes the turning direction. I found this out

I watched as his pride burst into a sneer.

"I just got the coach, so it was the previous owner who didn't maintain them," I said.

His ego deflated like a punctured balloon as he grunted.

Realizing I was miffed, he changed his tune.

He didn't seem to be paying much attention to the back jack. I reminded him again about its popping up routine after extension. "Sometimes it takes a few minutes before it pops up."

He seemed to listen in an ignoring sort of way. I watched, hoping the jack would perform its little maneuver. Many attempts later, the jack continued to kick downward and extend straight to the ground. I felt like a parent who had rushed her feverish child to the doctor and upon the sight of the thermometer, the child's fever was gone. Upon the sight of the mechanic, the jack was working.

Tim continued to work the jacks up and down, giving them enough silicone to oil a battleship. I for one, was not sold on the fact that the real cause for the malfunction had been discovered. It seemed too simple. Watching the ritual, I realized I had driven thirty miles for nothing more than a spray job. To complete the conversation, he told me that the jacks were performing as designed. No more questions or suggestions would be entertained.

As I drove out of the parking lot, the side-view mirror began its journey toward the driver's door. I doubled back into the lot. Tim approached the motor home with a quizzical look on his face when he saw me.

"Sorry to bother you again, but I have this mirror that keeps moving toward the door. Could you take a quick look and tell me if the door has to come off to fix it?"

Tim laughed, looked at the elbow of the mirror, and walked into his shop. Seconds later he was back, asking me where I wanted the mirror. He inserted a small Allen wrench, twisted it and smiled.

In amazement, I asked, "That's all it took?"

"Yap!" he said. "No big deal."

"But I was told the door had to come off."

"Not hardly," was his jovial reply.

Although I wasn't particularly comfortable with the jacks being trouble-free, at least the trip wasn't a total waste. I knew how to make one more repair and I could scratch the mirror off my list.

The mirror held its ground, and the jacks would have to prove their reliability. With this latest adventure, I questioned if anyone in the business had the right answers.

Isn't it amazing that the tech in Richmond didn't know about the mirrors? And what about the jacks? Even if spraying them wasn't the cure-all, why didn't the tech offer it as a possibility, before sending me to Green Bay? Scary!

Chapter 16

The second set of temporary plates on the camper were about to expire. Not hearing from the dealership, I called to see what had happened. As usual, I listened to the same set of button pushing directions. This time I actually got a person. Connie told me the dealership had not received the vendor's copy of the title from the state. She said she couldn't do any about it..

"Could you please get another extension, so I can leave for Minnesota? My brother isn't doing very well. I need to be on my way."

"No," Connie snapped. "That won't work. We've already issued as many temporary plates as allowed by law."

Two months had lapsed, they had plenty of time to secure the title. My attitude bristled. I suggested a call to the license bureau should be made. She'd try and call me back the next day.

When she didn't call, I called her. Frustrated, I followed the commands. At least this time, I had some idea of which buttons to push. The phone rang and rang. When no one answered, I was routed back through the same menu, starting over with the same commands. Three trips around this block, and my patience had vanished.

Suddenly, a woman's voice interrupted my thoughts.

"This is Connie. Can I help you?"

"Yes, I'm calling about the title and plates for the motor home."

Carolee O'Neill

"Oh yes, I was about to call you. The license bureau is going to send the title out in the morning. It will take about a week to get it, but as soon as it gets here, I'll overnight it to you."

Feeling she had tried, I thanked her and hung up.

The week passed with no news. I tried to be patient, but the situation with my brother was growing grave. I waited a couple more days. When my plates expired, I called again. Reaching Connie, I got a reply which left me dumbfounded.

"I'm sorry, but I misplaced your phone number and I didn't know how to reach you."

"Why didn't you call the sales department to get my number?"

"We're all separate departments here," she said.

I wanted to say, "So they don't have a phone?" Her comment made no sense to me, but getting nasty wouldn't get the plates any faster either. I repeated the phone number and address. I asked her to read it back to me to be sure it was correct.

The title would be in the overnight mail in the morning.

On this note, I began preparing the motor home for its journey to Minneapolis. It would be my first trip with the motor home, an eight or nine hour drive. My brother's family would come for a visit. Of course, they would all want to see the camper.

When I awoke the next morning, gray skies had given way to heavy rains. My granddaughters didn't seem to mind as they donned their rain gear. I

78

watched as the three of them walked haphazardly down the drive to catch the school bus. I had to laugh. Katie, the youngest, didn't miss too many puddles.

Playing in the rain had to be an inherited gene. When it wasn't lightning, my mom let us play in the rain in our sun-suits. I remember the ends of my bangs sending streams of water down my face and the prickle of cool raindrops bouncing off my skin. It felt so good, especially after a grueling day behind my desk in grade school. If we were really lucky, we didn't have an umbrella along on rainy days. Mom wouldn't scold because we had a good excuse for being soaked. I wondered if Mom hadn't done the same thing as a child because she never got very upset when we dripped all over the cubbyhole floor.

Now the little wooden house at the end of the drive would serve its purpose. It had been built for just such occasions to keep the children warm and dry. Of course, nobody could calculate the damage puddles or snowball fights would cause along the way. As I watched them from the window of the motor home, I didn't see anyone banned from entry or a body flying out of the door. They managed somehow—through the grace of the good Lord.

The day became tiresome as I ran back and forth between the coach and the house to let the dogs out. By lunchtime the water had topped the soles of my shoes, making its way inside to soak my socks. I continued to look out of the camper's front window to be sure I wouldn't miss the FedEx truck.

What a relief it would be to cross something else off my list. Connie told me the delivery would be made before four in the afternoon. With the vendor's title in hand I could pick up the plates in the morning and leave for Minnesota.

Four o'clock came and went, but the title never made it. As time was of the essence, I called again the next morning. Upset with the command pushing system, I wondered if any companies ever used people. As it was a mute point, I prepared myself for the conversation with Connie.

Perhaps she missed the pickup time. Maybe she was ill. I have to give her the benefit of the doubt.

A sigh of relief escaped when I finally reached her. The letter had gone out on schedule.

"I'm surprised you don't have it by now," she said.

"Don't you have a tracking number? You can use it to call FedEx to locate the letter."

"I don't have time to do that today. I'm sure you'll have it by tomorrow," she said with a snippy tone in her voice.

"I insist. Otherwise, you can transfer me to your supervisor."

Within the hour she called me with another unbelievable message.

"I mistakenly put the wrong zip code on the envelope. The letter is someplace in Michigan."

"You did what?"

The repeated errors had replaced my patience with my boiling point.

"I'm sorry, there's nothing I can do."

"Oh yes there is," I said. "You'll call FedEx with your tracking number and give them the incorrect and the correct zip code, so they can locate the letter."

"Like I said, I don't have any more time to chase this down," she argued.

"You have detained me for days because of your inefficiency and errors. I expect that out of decency you will locate the letter. Otherwise, I'm going to speak to your supervisor."

Later that day, when I was out in the motor home, Connie called and made the mistake of talking to my daughter-in-law.

Teresa, a tall, stunning blonde, worked in a management position at a major paper mill. Thinking for some insane reason Teresa would side with her.

"She shouldn't have left home until she had the title. Then she wouldn't be sitting in your driveway," Connie said.

Knowing what had transpired, Teresa set the record straight. As for me, I wondered why Connie thought people bought campers—to stay home?

The FedEx truck arrived late the next day with the letter. The edges were torn and shredded after its long journey, but I didn't care. I had it and that's all that mattered. The delivery man told me one of the guys in Michigan happened to notice the address didn't coincide with the zip code. He made the correction and voila, the delivery was made. I thanked him and his company for doing a great job.

He smiled and said, "That's what we're here for, ma'am."

I laughed as I thought about what Paul Harvey would've said, "If he only knew the rest of the story!"

Chapter 17

As I rounded the bend on highway fifteen, going toward Mound, Minnesota, glistening waters sparkled their delight. The countryside laid claim to rich green hillsides that dipped down to cross lakes and rivers like the Saint Croix and the Mississippi. Getting closer to my brother's, every curve revealed a phenomenal view of Lake Minnetonka. Its watery branches flowed through the hills of the countryside like a spider weaving a web. One could have a grand view of the lake and all of its activities for the price of a meal at the Minnetonka Mist. Sailboats appeared as butterflies with uncharted patterns over the lake's choppy surface.

The waters of the Arkansas River looked much the same the year we took our twenty-six foot fifth wheel to Colorado. David and my son Chris, who was David's gold mining buddy, apparently didn't think the river looked ominous. I did. I suggested they check with the Chamber to learn about the currents.

"That's not necessary," they agreed, looked at each other and laughed.

"Just drop us off up the mountain and we'll ride the river back to the van," Chris said.

As I looked into the eyes of Daisy, a liver and white Springer Spaniel, I swear she had a pleading look on her face that said, — "Do I have to go with them?" As Daisy went everywhere with Chris, there wasn't a chance she'd get out of this ride.

Chris's lean, muscular body glistened as he lowered the canoe down the eight-foot bank to David. We said our goodbyes and I took off for Colorado Springs to visit my friend, Phyllis. When I got home, I found two "glad to be alive" fellows sitting in the camper.

Fear lit Chris's crystal blue eyes as he told their story with all the wildest gyrations and in lightning speed. David nodded to Chris' rendition as he sat on the sofa without a word.

"As soon as we were in the canoe, the current slammed us against a boulder. David was in the back and I was in the front. I don't know about mine, but David's paddle was bowed from the pressure. We tried everything, but we couldn't turn the canoe.

Daisy was standing on the seat, doing a balancing act. I never thought I'd see panic in my dog's eyes, but it was there, Mom. She kept looking back and forth between the two of us, whining.

The freezing water began filling the canoe. We were drenched! We finally got free, but not for long!" He shouted. "This time we slammed crosswise into the next bunch of boulders. We were stuck, but good.

Daisy saw her chance and jumped to shore," Chris laughed heartily. "The dog had more sense than we did. We decided to follow her lead, but it took a lot of muscle to get there. I left David to hang on to the canoe while I went for the van. Then I realized it was five miles down the road.

I couldn't believe it. Nobody would give me a ride. Not even the guys who drove those rafting

buses. When I got back to David, I had to get the
canoe up the bank and onto dry land. Just then a
guide with a rafting group went by and yelled,
'You're not going to try this river in a canoe, are
you? Two guys tried that yesterday in kayaks and
one of them is dead.' Can you imagine, Mom?
Dead! Sure wish he would've come by before we
tried it! You can't believe how bad the current
was."

As I glance across the lake, I chuckled.
*Hindsight is a marvelous learning tool. It's no
wonder mothers grow gray prematurely.* It wouldn't
be long now, maybe five more miles to Brother
Bob's.

Stately trees cloaked brother's all-cedar
home that sat high on a private hillside, overlooking
one of the smaller branches of the lake. The
outreaching limbs had formed a tunnel- like
opening to veil their narrow blacktop drive. The
entrance would be much more of a challenge than
Greg's. Thankful for previous experience, I made
the turn. Bob sat on the front porch in his lawn
chair, bent forward with his elbows resting on his
knees. A few strands of dark-brown hair had been
pulled over the top of his head to hide his baldness.
His wife, Cherrie, a tall, robust woman, stood next
to him. Upon seeing me, she waved a hearty hello.
A workman, with shovel in hand, dug a few feet in
front of the porch. With vigilance, the job for the
rock garden would be supervised.

*Typical engineer has to make sure the job is
done right!* The wood-shingled roof dipped down to
an overhang along the front two-thirds of the house,

covering the porch. Potted plants and lawn furniture added the feeling of happy family gatherings. For now it was a place to do business. The evergreens along the front porch had suffered a bad case of winter kill.

Hearing the coach pull into the drive, Bob lifted his head. He looked thin and pale. He waved and smiled his elfish little grin that had become his hallmark and went back to supervising.

The workman heaved the shovel into the rocks, looked at Bob and shook his head. Wiping his forehead with the back of his arm, he replaced the small cap that sheltered his gleaming skin from the sun and went on to finish the job.

During dinner, we discussed the agenda for my visit. Bob's family would come to say hello. We'd go to an audiologist in Plymouth, Minnesota, for an adjustment on my hearing aids. There'd be trips to the hospital for Bob's chemotherapy, maybe a lunch or two, and, of course, we'd tour the motor home.

The visit, like life, ended too quickly. We played games, rested and watched "Wheel of Fortune." In between times, I listened to my brother's advice on traveling with a motor home. It was a bittersweet time, hugs shared, but final goodbyes were never spoken.

I stopped at the end of the drive, waving my final goodbye. Leaves rustled in the crisp air. It seemed early for fall to be harvesting its brilliance. For now the dusk of their lives would end until a new bond would be formed in the spring. It wouldn't be long before they would be sleeping under a blanket of snow.

* * *

My fiftieth class reunion didn't bring a round of applause for the senior driving a motor home. After the initial shock of learning about my escapades, only one person wanted to see it. She had been my best friend in high school. I'd never know if she was being kind or really interested.

As the last several years of my life had been filled with trauma, I hadn't been to the opera nor had I spent time with my grandchildren. I had little to share with my classmates other than the beginnings of my new adventure. Since they showed little interest in that, I spent the weekend smiling politely, listening to melodious noise from the constant chatter. Understanding was impossible, not to mention exhausting. It didn't take long before the commotion caused me to lose interest in their conversations. I had joined them in their disinterest.

I would spend the night alone, parked in the lot behind the hotel. I didn't have a twinge of fear. Perhaps I was too numb from David's death, the lessons with the motor home, and the preparations of the last few months.

After a day and a half of chatter, I decided to change plans and leave right after the luncheon on Saturday. We said our goodbyes, hugging and giggling like school girls. The thought that the next time we met we could very well be in another dimension, crossed my mind. I left with the anticipation that before this happened, I was going to see the country.

Chapter 18

When I called the dealership for an appointment, I thought Ben, the service manager, would have a heart attack.

"Oh no, ma'am! We're booked solid for the next two weeks. I don't know why maintenance told you all I needed was a week. I'll have to see what I can move round and call you back. Sorry about this."

I continued to move forward with my plans even though I wasn't sure what would happen. As it turned out, Ben squeezed my work into his schedule somehow. I couldn't wait to roll.

My escapades began a little before seven in the morning, on a very cold November 12, 2002. Puffy gray clouds filled the sky, hanging low in the distance. The weather forecast predicted sleet, unusual, but not unlikely at this time of the year. The coach didn't need much preparation.

The trips to Minnesota and Milwaukee took care of that. I had to check a few things, like making sure the canvas around the bike had been tied securely. With a little luck, an early start would put me south of the storm before it hit Indiana. Even so, my fingers had already begun to burn from the cold. In spite of the nip in the air my spirits were high. I would soon be on my way to the dealership in Richmond for the repairs. As I pulled myself into the driver's seat, the thought of my long awaited adventure rang clear.

I turned the cab heater on high to warm my hands as soon as I started the motor. The blast of cold air joined my shivered. I never expected a storm so early in November. Like all humans, I blamed the dealership for not delivering the license plates sooner. *I would've been gone by now and not worrying about freezing to death.*

The dealership in Richmond had a campground where I could stay until the repairs were done. I could always read the manual again while I waited, boring, but necessary. Maybe I'd learn something this time.

I went to the service department as soon as I arrived. Ben told me that the repairs would take two days, and the fellows would start them the next morning at eight sharp. He asked that I have the camper outside the bay doors by that time. I handed Ben the list of repairs. Surprised, he sat down to read them.

See Appendix 7: Dealership: RV Questions/Repairs.

"I see you have some things on here that haven't been authorized," he said as he continued to read.

"Like what?"

"Well, the antenna for one thing. And I'm not sure about the toilet. I'll have to check with our sales manager to see what he is willing to do. In the meantime, we'll start on the things I know we can do."

"I have a letter from your sales manager, stating the company is willing to install the antenna."

"This will make it much easier," he said. Then I mentioned a few things that I wanted done, like additional outlets to use for a lamp, a Christmas tree and the battery charger.

After settling as much as we could, I walked across the parking lot toward the camper. A chill in the air told me summer had slipped into winter, bypassing much of the fall.

The weather is sure a lot different than the last time I was here. At the closing the sun forced every drop of moisture out of my body.

I turned when I heard a voice behind me.

"Follow me, ma'am," a young man hollered. "I'll guide you to the campground."

"Sounds good," I yelled as I got into the motor home.

Although I had dodged the storm on the way down, the clouds were beginning to look rather ominous to the northwest. They had changed direction to a southerly course.

The campground was a row of sites in a parking lot that offered no protection from the weather. I needed to get settled as soon as possible. The young man guided me into my space and hooked up my sewer and electric. He did the job in a matter of minutes. It would have taken me over a half an hour. Because of the freezing temperatures, he put four gallons of water into the fresh-water tank, instead of hooking up the hose.

"Don't worry about disconnecting things in the morning. I'll be over to take care of it for you," he said.

"Are you sure?"

90

"Sure, I'd be glad to."

What a relief. All my imaginings had been of warm balmy breezes, never freezing fingers. The cold hard facts were I'd never get as good at setting up and breaking down the camper as my young man. Youth and guy muscles were on his side.

Later that evening, I relaxed in my nightgown on the loveseat. The weather had gotten much worse. I couldn't see what nature had planned with the blinds closed, and I wasn't going to peek. The furnace ran continuously, but the floor still felt cool to my bare feet. It wasn't going to be the warmest night of my life. Then the wind started a tapping sound. I assumed it was the plastic loop that hung from the awning being tossed against the side of the coach. A rattle joined the tapping as the wind forced the flap on the exhaust fan open and closed. I covered the bed with an extra blanket. Then I crawled between the cool sheets, allowing my Cuddle Ewe to warm my body.

A chill aroused me a couple of hours later. The top of my head and the end of my nose were uncomfortably cold. The strongest winds seemed to be hitting the window on the back wall of the camper.

As a teenager, I used to listen to the wind in my parents' two story stucco home. The sound sent me plunging under the covers to find some warmth in their darkness. Very little heat got to the second floor from the gravity furnace, no matter how high Mom turned the thermostat. My older brother used to say it was so cold that you could see the frost on the walls. I never saw it. I only noticed the frost on the windows because he had carved his initials on them, although I expected to see frost on the camper windows with the wind blowing so hard. I propped some pillows in front of the back window to detour the cold, and I slid deep under the covers. On my descent I decided that buying a space heater would be a good idea.

I had been awake for an hour before I decided to get up. Frigid air would greet me as I crawled out of bed. I wasn't disappointed as my foot touched the floor instead of my slipper. I grabbed my bathrobe as fast as I could. When I bent over to put my slippers on, I put my hand in front of the heat register to see if the furnace was running. I felt nothing. I walked as fast as I could toward the front of the coach. Alas, the living room wasn't much warmer.

The direction of the wind must be the problem.

The furnace responded with a blast of cool air up my nightgown when I turned the thermostat to seventy-five. My muscles tensed as I moved away from the register. After a moment the air began to warm and brought welcomed relief.

At least I wouldn't have to shower and get dressed in the cold.

I returned to the register in the bedroom, but nothing had changed. I jotted my "lack of heat" on a piece of paper for Ben. As I raised the bedroom blinds I saw that the windows were packed with snow. I couldn't expect the technician to help me with these conditions. The dealership would have him busy with other jobs, like clearing roads.

92

Breaking down the unit would be an interesting task for me. I had no idea where the sewer hose had been connected, probably buried under one or maybe two feet of snow, and my personal belongings did not include a shovel or a pair of boots. I could grumble all I wanted, but I had the responsibility of getting the coach to the service department on time.

After looking out of the front window, I put on my warmest gear. Unable to see much, I ducked down and saw a foot and a half of piled snow sitting on the hood. Cone-shaped icicles were hanging from the edges above the cab doors, dipping down to touch the snow. Evergreen branches drooped from their heavy white burden as sparrows and black birds sought shelter in their boughs. Deep ruts from heavy equipment surrounded the campground, the kind that struck terror in a driver.

Like a child, I stood in awe of the picturesque setting. My adventure had begun. A brisk Christmas morning would be like this: billowy snowflakes floating aimlessly to the ground, colorfully wrapped gifts tied together with satin ribbons, the smell of fresh cut pine. There was time to look, to see, and to enjoy.

My eyes caught a glimpse of a figure approaching the coach dressed in a heavy blue parka and wearing high boots. It was the young man who had offered his help.

I opened the door to greet him. He squinted as he looked up at me.

"Are you ready to get moving, ma'am?"

"Indeed I am," I replied, more pleased than he would ever know.

Chapter 19

Ben had asked me to go through the coach to show him what I wanted done. This way there wouldn't be any mistakes.

"Several of these repairs were things the Pre-Delivery Department should have taken care of before the coach left the dealership. I'm sorry about that," Ben said.

Foremost in my mind was the transmission fluid for the jacks and the slide. The containers were both found to be bone dry. Concerned that these systems could have been damaged, I asked Ben if he would call the manufacturers. He assured me that if the tech couldn't get the jacks to work according to the way they were designed, he'd call Hydraulic Leveling Corporation (HWH). He wasn't concerned about the slide as it had only been used once.

"We'll check the fluid levels and fill the tanks. Then we'll run the slide and the jacks a few times to lubricate them well. That should do the trick," he said.

See Appendix 4: Pre-Delivery Instructions-Used.

While they continued to do my work, I visited with folks who were waiting for repairs. With a matter-of-fact attitude, they told me, "Even new coaches need repairs. That's the way it is in RV land. You might as well get used to it."

Their stories were disheartening. Seals weren't properly installed. Exit doors wouldn't stay closed during travel. Hydraulics weren't functioning right. It didn't matter the brand or size of the units; they all had problems. The coach had to be used as much as possible so the repairs would surface before the warranty expired. My camper's warranty had already run out. Thankfully, the sales manager agreed to complete mine at no charge.

The service department wasn't the most comfortable place to spend time. The ins and outs of the staff kept the room drafty, and the concrete floor kept my feet cold. The two days for repairs mushroomed into five because they didn't have a part for the toilet. The technician tried to convince me the toilet worked fine the way it was; it didn't need water in it.

"Excuse me!" I disagreed.

When that didn't work, he said it could take days to get the part. As much as I wanted to be out of there, I stayed with the plan.

"I don't think so," I said. "This is the third unit I've owned and the first two had water in the toilet. As a nurse I want water in my toilet. So I suggest you get on the phone and overnight the part."

He stared at me with a curious, twisted look on his face. I was sure he wondered what nursing had to do with water in the toilet. He didn't argue, I got my way. After all, I am a blonde.

The black water valve was the only repair Ben couldn't get authorized. However, he said he'd have the technician work the valve stem back and forth, so it wouldn't pull so hard. More silicone, I assumed. The bedroom was as warm as it was going to get. It was too far from the furnace.

The technician's shirt buttons almost popped off when he shared his discovery. "There wasn't any transmission fluid in the container for the jacks," he said.

I didn't tell him we already knew this.

"I filled it so they should be fine now."

I thought about what he said and then it dawned on me that Tim, the fellow in Green Bay, didn't know about the jacks, either. I couldn't resist asking Ben about the jacks needing to be sprayed with silicone.

"They don't need anything but transmission fluid. That's what keeps them lubricated. When you bring the coach in for a checkup always ask to have the hoses checked to make sure you aren't losing any fluid. Otherwise, you're fine."

Ben had worked hard to satisfy my needs. I'd have to call HWH if I wanted to know more about the jacks.

The day finally arrived when the coach was finished. Not really understanding everything, but acting like I did, I told Ben I wanted to check out the repairs with him. I didn't want to find unsatisfactory repairs five hundred miles down the road. He agreed.

The inspection completed, I drove the coach to an area that wasn't level. I needed to know the jacks were working properly. After several minutes of pushing the arrows, I had gotten all the jacks to come down except the back one. It continued to be temperamental. I told Ben and he came to the coach. Of course, the jack worked like a charm. Disgruntled, I moved the coach. As I did, I noticed a large puddle of transmission fluid on the pavement. I sighed and drove back to the service department.

When I found Ben, he said, "That's normal. The tech more than likely put too much fluid in the box. Just make sure you have the level checked when you get south."

The box for the transmission fluid was halfway under the coach. I'd have to find someone to crawl underneath it. Even if I did attempt it, I wouldn't be able to unscrew the cap. Men always give a connection an extra twist which means, "It's on there forever." Besides, with the fluid on the ground I needed to be sure the box hadn't been punctured, before they filled it. Staying overnight in their campground would give me an opportunity to work with the jacks, see if I lost any fluid overnight, make sure the toilet held water, use the new antenna they installed and the plug. If everything checked out, I could get a decent start the next morning.

That evening a big rig pulled in alongside of my camper. As I've heard how friendly campers are, I decided to see what my neighbor had to say about my puddle.

"Sounds like the tech checked the transmission fluid with the jacks down," he said. "You have to check the fluid with the jacks up because it's a closed system, like a car. When the jacks are extended the fluid will register low. So if he put the fluid in and then raised the jacks the pressure would cause the fluid to ooze out from under the cap on the box. I bet that's where your puddle came from."

"Now that makes sense. Thanks for the info. I'll sleep much better because of it."

The expertise of all the technicians was really in question now.

The first tech didn't know an Allen wrench would solve the problem with the traveling mirror. The next one tried to talk me out of fixing the toilet. Of course Tim, the fellow in Green Bay, wasn't successful with the jacks, either. Did the tech really understand how the jacks were supposed to function? If he did, why did he put fluid in the box when the jacks were down? This scenario made me crazy.

I wondered if my repairs had been completed competently. I wanted to give them the benefit of the doubt. Ben had given me his full attention, even though he had to squeeze me into the schedule. Perhaps they were in too much of a hurry to put the jacks up—a minor detail to him. Yet the thoughts of what the fellow in the waiting room said rang clear, "That's the way it is in RV land. You might as well get used to it."

After five days of listening to people complain about their rigs and sitting on plastic chairs that should've been awarded the "backache seat of America," I was happy to be on my way to Atlanta for Thanksgiving.

My next stop after that would be Venice, Florida for Christmas. When I called Nickie, David's sister-in-law, she asked if I wanted to spend the winter parked at her home. She said she had the perfect spot. She and her deceased husband used to have a motor home so she knew exactly what I'd need. I'd have water and electric. I could use the bathroom in the house and that would keep my tanks from filling too fast. Excited about the invitation, I accepted the offer. It would save me a bundle.

Chapter 20

Driving down the narrow street that mid-afternoon, I looked for my perfect spot. Tall, bushy evergreens hovered close to the roadway. A queasy feeling told me I might be in for an unpleasant surprise. As I stopped in front of the house, I noticed the sloped yard. The coach would be difficult to level and I didn't see a good place to park, except in front of the garage. That would block access to it. The pines had been sporadically planted around the yard, which left very little room to park a wide body motor home. I stopped on the road to see if Nickie had something better planned than what I had imagined.

After a casual greeting, Nickie assured me her brother Ted could get the camper between the pines. He had sold RV's and could get them into small spaces.

My stomach did a flip flop when I remembered the time David had taken the Mountain Aire in for repairs. He handed the keys to a salesperson, who took a corner too sharp, and tore the awning. The salesman denied the incident and David couldn't remember if he had hit anything recently. So we ended up splitting the cost with the dealership.

Being Nickie's guest, I tried to ignore the scraping sounds of the branches as Ted squeezed the camper between the evergreens. Nickie stood motionless in a light pink sweat suit, arms folded under her breast. Her black hair, with occasional streaks of gray, accented her pale complexion and solemn features.

With the camper parked, I'd have to level it. I didn't hear an offer to help with the job. For assurance, I read the manual again and it reminded me to always bring the back jacks down first, not possible. With the slope of the land they hit the ground almost immediately, so much for help from the manual.

My attention then shifted to the front jacks. *Something is bound to work but the way things are going, I'm not too sure about that.*

Pushing the control button I got my answer. They weren't going to clear the ground either.

Call me a pessimist, if you will, but I sure called this one right. I'll have to get permission from Nickie to dig out the dirt from in front of them.

Nickie felt her small gardening tool would suffice for the job. After a, "You're kidding me" thought, which was seen only from within, I began to dig on the concrete-like dirt to get it as flat as possible. After an hour and a half it looked like the chocks were level. I lowered the jacks. An indescribable joy bound through every cell of my body as they made a solid connection. I sat in the dirt just as proud as David was after he finished washing and waxing our thirty-eight foot fifth wheel.

Brushing myself off, I went into the camper to clean up. As I turned the water on, I hesitated.

I can't use too much water or my tank will fill up. I'll have to ask Nickie where I can empty the gray water, maybe in the backyard. I sure don't

*want to move the coach unless it is absolutely
necessary.*

I chuckled as an mischievous thought ran
through my head.

*I could never use the kitchen sink or the
bathroom in the RV. Then I wouldn't have to empty
anything. I can just wander back and forth to the
house whenever necessary.*

My chuckle turned into a grimace as my
stupid notion reminded me that I could be tripping
over tree limbs in the dark or fighting off huge
Florida bugs that ended up in my hair, just to use a
bathroom. With the lay of the land, my crystal ball
showed there would be more digging in my future
and I'd still be wearing a path from the coach to the
house.

Chapter 21

Although the chocks helped, the unit wasn't level. I couldn't raise the nose any further or the jacks would be hyper-extended and the front tires would be off the ground. Within a week, my lower back and legs went into spasms. Time would tell how long I could tolerate my perfect spot.

The camper hid in the evergreens about fifty yards from Nickie's back door. On every visit, bar none, a little barking dog announced my arrival. He refused to acknowledge that I belonged to the premises. The dog's high-pitched bark, amplified by my hearing aids, traveled the auditory route and sent blows of sharp pain to my nervous system. Nothing I could do would silence him. Talking to him, petting him, nothing soothed his ruffled disposition. I began to wonder how much a muzzle would cost.

About a week later, I discovered my beautiful coach had become infested with ants. I approached Nickie with this distressing news. Her reply, shall I say, was rather abrupt.

"You can't expect to come to Florida and not have ants!"

With the tone of that comment, obviously little, if any, help would be forthcoming. The battle against these unwelcome guests, who seemed to be coming and going according to the menu, was mine alone. Not having any detour signs they'd pay attention to, I borrowed Nickie's car and headed to the hardware store. Arming myself with ant destruction tools, the strategy would be to spray

everything in sight, outside and inside, place little
ant boxes inside the coach at various spots along
with an ant poison called Toro. Then I'd put all the
food stuff in the refrigerator.

Let's see them get in there!

My son suggested kitchen cleanser around
the jacks. By the time I finished the job, the jacks,
the water hose and the power cord were white.

There! That should get rid of them.

But it didn't. Those little critters weren't
about to give up their new home. They walked
around the edge of my drinking glass, swarmed
over the garbage, and even accompanied me to bed.

After I had used up most of my Toro, Nickie
said, "Toro only works on sweet eating ants. It
wouldn't work on the others."

How was I supposed to know which ants
had a sweet tooth?

No matter what I did, they marched in and
out of my domain. I decided to scout the outside
area again. I couldn't believe it. I was parked over a
huge ant hill. As luck would have it, Nickie said the
entire yard had been treated, except for—guess
where! Nickie giggled as I discussed this tidy piece
of information with her. Was I thrilled I had made
her day? About this time, I sat somewhere between
speechless and the contemplation of a murderous
deed.

During my silent deliberation, I heard her
say, "You should be thankful that they aren't fire
ants."

That did it. Outnumbered, one to a trillion, and the ants were winning, I decided that if they weren't leaving, I would.

The next morning, Ted came over and asked how things were going.

"Not good! I'm infested with ants."

"That shouldn't be a problem," he said. "My sister has a bag of treated woodchips that will get rid of them right away."

Disbelief silenced my vocal chords as I stood with my mouth open.

Nickie and her brother Morton had inherited their parents' home. However, as they didn't get along they felt the best solution would be to divide the house. Then they could each live in their own half. This left Nickie without a kitchen unless she wanted to use her brother's.

A small room off her living room had been jam-packed with items necessary for a kitchen, a dining room and a computer room. She managed her meals with a microwave, a Dutch oven and some George Foreman products. The thought that sanitation could be a concern, as she washed and dried her dishes in the small bathroom, never crossed her mind. It did mine. Watching her stack the wet dishes on the lid of the toilet kept me eating my meals in the camper or looking for a paper plate.

With Christmas a breath away, I invited Nickie to my home for Christmas dinner. I had packed my Christmas dishes and glassware for the trip so I could have a guest and fuss for the holidays. My little tree stood lit on the front shelf, joined by other Christmas decorations scattered throughout the coach. I was all set. After seeing my dishes and stemware, Nickie decided we would have dinner at her place. She instructed me to bring my dishes and the food to her house, like a command from a drill sergeant. She would invite her brothers, especially the one she didn't get along with.

Trying to consider the giving nature of the holidays, I carried dishes, glassware, and extra food, wondering where I'd put them once I got to her home. Luckily, her non-social brother allowed us to use the oven in his kitchen for the Cornish hens and other Christmas delicacies. After several invitations had been extended to the other half of the household, and smelling the food for hours, Morton decided to come for a quick look and left. Ted, the brother who parked the camper, didn't mind. He ate his brother's share, without concern.

After the meal, it took several trips to get the dirty dishes back to the camper. For some reason, I couldn't bring myself to wash everything in her bathroom. In the end, Christmas turned into a job laden with extra chores and very little joy to the world. I wanted out of there, yesterday. Somehow, I would have to prepare myself and be as cordial as possible for a departure.

Part of the preparation would be to dump my black and gray water tanks as they were full. So I asked Ted where I could dump the coach.

"There's a campground about fifteen miles away. It's a little far, but they are the cheapest. The rest of them are twice as much."

The next morning, I went to the house to tell Nickie I planned to leave for the campground. As usual, she had the phone to her ear and ignored my motions. So I left, thinking she'd figure it out.

There were two dump sites at the campground: one with ankle deep mud and the other with no water. I always carried about three gallons of fresh water that I could use to flush the tanks. That wouldn't do a very good job, but it was better than nothing.

After I got the valves on the unit lined up with the dump site, I began putting on my rubber gloves. I noticed a short, pudgy gentleman headed my way. A baseball cap attempted to hide his bald head, but the holes revealed his secret. He looked harmless enough; however, his furrowed brow told me something might be wrong. By the time he got within thirty feet of me, that all changed. His face blossomed into a good-humored smile.

"Do you need any help?" he asked. "My name is Henry."

"No thank you, Henry. I think I have it under control."

He turned and pointed across the empty campground toward a coach. "Me and the missus are in the big fifth wheel over there."

"Nice rig. Are you full-timers?"

"No, we're just out here for a couple of days. If it stays cold we'll probably head toward Fort Myers. Are you sure you don't need any help?"

"I'm sure. But thanks anyway."

Silence lingered as he stood with his hands tucked in his jean pockets. My technique for emptying the tanks needed some polish next to that of an experienced RV'er, so I became uncomfortable with his watchfulness. As the seconds passed, I realized Henry intended to stay for the whole show. He hadn't budged an inch, so I proceeded as though I knew what I was doing.

I managed to get the cap off of the valve without the hammer. I said a little prayer of thanksgiving. I hooked up the sewer hose to the valve and placed the other end in the dump sewer. My confidence grew with each step accomplished. I paused for a moment to look at Henry. His eyes had saddened.

"Is something wrong?" I asked.

Shifting his weight, he said, "I have to help you with something. When you drove in my wife saw you get out of the cab. When she realized you were alone, she told me to get out here and help you," he chuckled. "I knew I'd better hop right to it if I knew what was good for me. There's got to be something I can do."

"How very kind of her! Tell her thanks for me. Come to think of it, there is something. I'm going to have to flush my black water tank, but the water valve at this dump site is turned off. I don't see a water connection that is close enough to reach from here. Do you happen to know where there is one?"

"Oh, I have lots of hose, maybe a hundred feet. I can hook it up to one of the campsites and run it over to you." Almost skipping, he hurried back to his camper.

I waited until I saw Henry coming back.

Sure hope I can get this valve open. I don't want to put on a show like I did at Greg's.

Positioning myself, I grabbed the black water valve and tugged as I bent into a squatting position. I couldn't budge it. Seeing me struggle, Henry offered his muscle. I didn't refuse. He pulled on the valve until he got red in the face.

"Something's wrong with this valve," Henry said. "It shouldn't be that hard to open. Sometimes toilet paper gets stuck in them and it doesn't take much of it."

"It's been like that since I bought the coach.

"No...no, something is wrong. There's an RV service center just down the road a piece. Take it over there and see what they can do."

After several tries, Henry got the valve open. He sprayed the steel stem on the valve with some silicone and worked it back and forth. When he had finished, a broad smile crossed his face. He looked as pleased as a fellow pulling on his suspenders with his thumbs.

After the tanks were flushed, Henry began to coil the hose into a circle. "Always make sure you disconnect your hose at the faucet first, so you don't get a back flush from the black water tank. Well, I'd better be heading back. Pleasure to meet you, ma'am."

"Thanks so much, Henry. I couldn't have done it without you."

I watched him for a moment as he walked away. He turned one last time and hollered, "Drive safely now."

Carolee O'Neill

"I will, Henry, and thanks again. Don't forget to thank the missus for me."

After I put everything away, I looked skyward. Gray clouds moved across the sky, pushed by strong winds. I decided I'd better head back to Nickie's. The visit to the service center would have to wait until after the storm had passed.

Parked again in my perfect spot and worn out from the ordeal, I turned on the television. I snuggled into my pillow on the sofa, getting set for a good movie. Seconds later, lightning lit the sky as it snapped out its threat. A deep, throaty rumble echoed through the wind; no doubt a pretty strong storm was headed my way. Within a couple of minutes gusts of wind, accompanied by battering rain, caused the coach to sway to its rhythm. Another clap of lightning sounded. My gaze went toward the ceiling. A dark spot encircled the controls for the satellite dish. With the storm casting shadows, I got up to check it. A light touch to the carpeted ceiling told me I had a leak.

Please tell me I'm wrong! But if the tech had checked the seals in Indiana, I shouldn't have a leak.

In a split second my internal furnace had fired up to shoot flame-filled thoughts in the direction of the tech who had done the repairs. Then I reminded myself of everything that went right.

However, my brain shouted, *Two-bits says he jerry-rigged the satellite dish to install the local antenna and never resealed it.*

I couldn't do anything at that point except pray the rain would stop. Lightning answered my prayer with another loud clap. It looked like I would be up all night, trying to soak up as much water as possible. In spite of my efforts, the stain gradually spread to cover about fifty percent of the ceiling in the kitchen and dinette area.

A couple of hours later the rain stopped, but the stain continued to broaden. The muscles in my arms and upper back had stiffened from patting the ceiling with towels. After several hours, I gave up. Exhaustion sent me to bed with a number ten headache. All I could do was hope the rain had stopped for the rest of the night.

The next day, I drove to the RV service center Henry suggested. After I squeezed the camper between some coaches, I walked into the office. A man stood at a computer by the front desk. His face, a blank stare, gave the impression that the computer owned him. He continued to type, never taking his eyes off the screen.

Regardless, I explained, "From what I've read and heard, the two things an RV'er doesn't want to deal with are a leaky ceiling and a black water valve that won't open. Lucky me! I have both."

He didn't relinquish the computer screen as he said, "Take a seat and a technician will do an inspection as soon as the shop can spare someone."

Within a half hour I got the news, "We don't have a valve to replace yours, ma'am. You'll have to put in an electric one. That will run you about two hundred dollars, unless we can't get that one to fit. If it doesn't, it'll be around three hundred dollars. The good news is you won't have this problem anymore. As for the leak, well, whoever caulked around the satellite dish caulked over mildew. Caulking just won't stick to mildew, ma'am."

Three hundred and fifty dollars later, I drove back to the house.

Chapter 22

The camper was back in its spot at Nickie's, hugging the evergreens. Dead tired and dirty, I washed the best I could, but I really wanted to fall into bed. As I planned to leave in the morning, I'd have to take care of a few things. Envelopes needed to be addressed and posted for my mail. Nickie would only have to insert the mail and seal the envelope. Finished with the task, I walked over to the house. To my surprise, I found the door locked, but the dog was still barking. I waited until Nickie opened the door.

She snarled, "You'd better go check your email."

Surprised by the comment, I said, "I'll have to come in to do that."

"Well, you're not coming in!" she snapped.

"Then I can't check my email. I've been checking my email in your home since I got here. I don't have a phone line in the camper, remember?"

Even though I'd been in her trees and tromping through her house the last month, the look on her face said this was a revelation.

"I just came over to tell you I'd be leaving in the morning. I brought you some stamped envelopes for my mail. As soon as I can, I will put a change of address in at the post office."

She grabbed the envelopes and slammed the door. For the life of me, I couldn't figure out what had upset her, nor did I get the opportunity to ask.

As I walked back to the camper, I tried to rationalize my stupidity.

I sure wish I had gone somewhere else for Christmas, anywhere. I wonder if she thought I had left without saying goodbye. I tried telling her I was going to take care of the camper, but she was on the phone again. Well, I can wonder from now until doomsday. If she's not going to talk to me, there's nothing I can do about it. I'll have to find a place to check my email. I'm sure that will give me all the details.

Although difficult, I tried not to allow her problem to become mine. That would take some doing because I have a tendency to want the world to like me.

Too bad we couldn't have parted as friends, especially since I have no desire to return.

To keep my mind off of getting the door slammed in my face, I busied myself in the motor home.

I'll be heading south very early in the morning, long before she'll be up. Probably before the ants are up. With any luck, the bumps in the road will shake the blasted critters right out of every crevice. Then I'll be rid of two problems, a trillion ants and my perfect spot.

* * *

Just before Christmas, I had made some reservations for myself at Bahia Honda, a state park in the Florida Keys. As I had left Nickie's earlier than expected, I had eight days before I could take advantage of their sandy beaches. I'd have to find a campground! I didn't want to spend that much time living in an empty lot.

I had planned the trip to the Keys as a "thank you" gift to Nickie for letting me stay in her bushes. After all that had happened, it was a good thing it didn't work out. Just before I got the last reservation, Nickie rearranged the agenda so often I lost several spots. First she wanted to go. Then she didn't. Her indecision confused my decisions. For some insane reason, I kept trying although I realized I must be a glutton for punishment. The final issue ended up being the dog. I tried to convince her to leave Fido behind. After all, we'd only be gone for a couple of days. She whined . . . Nickie, not the dog. The next moment I found her looking through the yellow pages for a kennel. Then she'd change her mind again. She called her brother, Ted. He didn't want anything to do with Fido.

She whimpered her concern, "What will I do with him? I can't send him to a kennel. Why...he could pick up something. I don't even want to think about that."

I understood because I never liked leaving my dog. Henry, my German shepherd, slept close and even sang with me when I played the piano. Let me assure you, as much as I like dogs, my wildest imaginings couldn't have come close to matching her plan.

In between Nickie's ambiguity, *she* decided on a solution for a doggie toilet. She'd strategically place diapers in the camper for the dog to do its duty. To say I panicked would be an understatement. My classy chassis could soon become a dumping ground for the dog. After a few deep breaths and a gulp I told her that wouldn't be

115

necessary. I'd be glad to stop when the dog needed a potty break.

"No," she said, as though I didn't have a choice. "I'll just put the diapers down."

Then I remembered the newspapers in the one corner of her house. I assumed Nickie collected them. This time I had the revelation. The dog, who had five years to get housebroke, had missed his training classes. My over-reactive imagination overreacted. Visions of the dog missing the diapers and going on the carpet struck a long sour note in my cranium. My stomach churned. I prayed for a nice way out of the mess, knowing I had created it.

I prayed again as I tried to make reservations with Nickie at my elbow. Even though I told her I'd take care of the finances, she had to know if there would be a charge for the dog. Fine! I'd do my best to find out. That didn't stop her; she continued to fire questions at me during the phone conversation, making understanding difficult. When I did reach the central office for the state parks in Florida, I was transferred to a ranger. I continued to pray for a miracle, wondering if I had worn God out yet. I posed the question about the dog and tried to control my elation when I heard him say, "The state parks don't allow dogs." Somehow, I maintained my composure. Nickie wouldn't leave without the dog. I had been saved, and all because I had gotten the answer to her question.

She didn't seem to be distressed over the lost trip, either. Picking up the dog, Nickie placed him in her lap. "I'm not going to leave you, sweetie.

You've always been there for me, and now I'm going to be there for you."

She began brushing his fuzzy, white hair aside with her hand and suddenly stopped short. I couldn't see what she was looking at with her head over the dog.

"Well, you won't be in there for long," she sneered. "I'll get my tweezers and pluck you right out of there."

"What is it?"

"Just a tick. I'll have to check her over to see if she has any more. The bushes are loaded with them."

This can't be happening! I'm not only parked over ants, but the place is full of ticks?

On a scale from one to ten, ticks are definitely a twelve for me. I had to deal with them in Maryland after finding them on the children and our dog. No thank you, I'll take the box-elder bugs any day of the week, before ticks.

Then I realized my good fortune as I said a prayer of thanksgiving. I didn't have to deal with the diapers or the ticks riding along with the ants.

The time had come to look to the future. Tired and with no place to go for the next few days, I pulled the camper into the darkened street just before dawn on December 31, 2002. I cringed as the evergreens dragged their branches across the sides of the coach for the last time. The "Mrs. Nice Person," who generally lived inside, needed a vacation. The struggle to understand communications with a hearing loss, the constant confusion from the never ending change in plans,

117

the sharp sting against my eardrums from the little dogs barking, the trips back and forth to the house for the bathroom, and trying to obey the house rules had taken their toll. However, the ants, the diapers, and the ticks had won first place.

As I drove toward the freeway, a panoramic view of a sunrise announced the new day. Its beginning glow cast a soft pink across the horizon. Layers of feather-like clouds streaked the sky, grabbing at the first hues of daylight. I thanked my heavenly Father for the privilege of this unforgettable vision, for the unforgettable time with Nickie and for the unforgettable lessons I had learned.

Chapter 23

Venice, Florida, was about an hour north of Fort Myers. I planned to put in a change of address as soon as I located a post office; I didn't want my mail lost or thrown away. I followed the road signs for the post office, anticipating a quick in, out and on my way. As I approached, I noticed a small parking lot on the west side of the building. Almost empty, it would be a safer place to park the camper. I went inside with my completed "Change of Address." The postal clerk assured me my mail would be forwarded to my daughter's starting the next day.

I pulled myself into the driver's seat and noticed an older truck had parked next to me. The truck would make exiting the lot a little trickier, but not impossible. I made my maneuver, relying on the image in the side mirror as to how much room I needed to clear the truck.

Ready to exit the lot, I noticed a young woman running toward the camper. I waited at the corner to see what she wanted. Maybe I had forgotten something or dropped something. I lowered the passenger's window.

"Ma'am, I hate to tell you this, but you just hit that man's pickup truck. The damage to the motor home is pretty bad. The bike looks like it is still secure so you should be able to drive."

Heat burned through my body; my heart banged.

I miscalculated maneuver.

I began to tremble as conflicting decisions flashed through my head.

Back up!

No! I can't do that. I'm on a one way street.

Maybe it's not as bad as she said.

I shouldn't be driving. Too late for that one.

I asked her to tell the man I would drive around the block and be back as soon as I could. I didn't look at the damage because I wouldn't have been able to drive around the block.

Get a grip, sister! You have to move this rig. You're on a one-way and traffic is hugging your backend.

At the exit the cross traffic sped by bumper to bumper as I waited for a break in traffic. Tears streamed down my checks until I couldn't see. Gripping the steering wheel with all my might, I told myself to take a deep breath and try to relax.

It's pointless to hurry. All it'll do is add another mistake. The fellow who owns the truck isn't going anywhere before I get back.

When I returned from my short, nerve-racking journey around the block, a man was standing with his family next to their vehicle.

My legs felt like jello that just started to thicken when my feet hit the pavement. As I walked toward the family with my back straight and my chin up, I prepared myself for the worst.

The man returned my greeting with a smile. "Howdy! My name is, John. Sure sorry about this. I can't believe it did that much damage. You just nicked my bumper."

"I'm very sorry. I thought I had enough room to clear."

"Well, you almost did. You needed…maybe another half inch."

I approached the older woman who I assumed was his wife and apologized for the mishap.

"The thing that's important is that nobody got hurt," she said.

While I was still rational, I asked John to show me the damage to his truck.

He pointed at the bumper. Amazingly, his bumper had only lost a little of its curve.

"We can exchange insurance information as soon as I look at the camper. I've already contacted American Family. My agent assured me everything would be taken care of."

As I walked to the back of the camper, I glanced into the glum faces of the family. I gasped as I cornered its backend.

A gaping hole displayed the skeletal construction. A see-saw diagonal tear went from the right bottom corner to the top of the coach on the opposite side. The steel bike rack had my bike in a grasp that twisted it upward with the front wheel turned outward. I didn't have to worry about looking for a campground. I wasn't going anywhere, except to the parking lot of an RV body shop.

Fiberglas had proven to be a poor contender against steel.

The body shop tried to accommodate my needs by allowing me to stay in the camper while the repairs were completed. I'm not sure if it was kindness or to get me out of the way while they overruled my company's request to hire their own adjustor. American Family didn't have an adjustor in Florida. Rather than lose time, the body shop said they would call one they always used. I could see the dollar signs changing right before my eyes.

The bid soared from three thousand to six thousand with the help of their adjustor. My insurance rate jumped right along with it. My little blunder had turned into an unplanned expense—a heavy-duty lesson on something I should've already learned—*always walk around the camper before moving it.*

In spite of my continued complaints about their procedure with the adjustor, they gave me an office upstairs with a phone line. I'd have a way to check my email and contact family. I almost laughed after opening the one from Nickie. I had never seen so many derogatory adjectives in one paragraph. Although she didn't say, it appeared that she thought I had left without a thank you or a goodbye.

The text did divulge the real reason for my invitation to stay on her property. She had planned to have some elective surgery. I was to be her private duty nurse, her captive caregiver. Self-serving, rude and inconsiderate were a few descriptions that filled the page.

An old adage says that you get more bees with honey than with vinegar. Or was it that you get

122

more caregivers with vinegar than with honey? As long as I was answering my email, I decided to complain to a friend about my perfect spot running aground. She reminded me of another old saying, "If it sounds too good to be true, it usually is."

Instead of paying for a campground, I had paid an emotional price, plus the additional cost of food and the five hundred dollar deductible on the insurance claim. I had put money before common sense with my first trip. I learned the hard way that everything comes with a price tag.

Carolee O'Neill

Chapter 24

The trip to the Keys, well, I was glad I did it, but I wouldn't do it again. Seventy-five miles into the peninsula the sandy beaches of the gulf occasionally became visible. Tall scraggly brush lined the well-worn road between the glimpses of the ocean. A parade of trucks and cars lumbered down the two-lanes that had few passing zones. There were plenty of pull-offs for sightseeing, but most of them combined the entrance and exit, leading the visitor into a narrow lot. Being caught in this situation, the driver would be forced to back up. As I had just had an expensive mishap, I wasn't going to attempt turning around between the ins and outs of fast moving tourists.

At Bahia Honda State Park, a Ranger would guide me into my space. Otherwise, I could be left to follow a snake-like trail drawn by a desk clerk on the back of a campground's brochure. A couple days rest, a little time to ride my bike, and a walk along the gulf was a welcomed thought.

My next reservation would be on Stock Island—ten miles east of Key West. As I traveled through the town, unkempt streets left a ghetto impression. Once through the park gates a different world emerged. The entrance, as one might suspect, had a tropical flare. The road split, surrounding a fountain of plunging waters. Rocks and palm trees were bordered by a variety of flowers on either side of the road. Rows of motor homes, which could be seen from the park's reservation office, had very little space between them. I asked the lady at the

124

front desk if someone could help me into my space.

"We don't have the staff for extra things. This park is for rest and relaxation," she said.

Being alone, backing the camper into a tight space meant numerous trips in and out of it to see how close I was to other rigs.

After at least thirty minutes and sweating off five pounds, the gal in the camper behind me came to my rescue. Liz, an easygoing person with happy eyes, a solid build and looked about fifteen years my junior, guided me like a pro. I had what I needed, beautiful weather, a nice space, a swimming pool and a bus to take me to Key West.

Set in my space, I went to hook up the water and electric. The RV dealership that installed the three hundred dollar electric valve didn't put the safety cap back on. That's the cap that I kept hitting with the hammer.

Looking at the valve Liz said, "It's remarkable how these so-called professionals can screw up, isn't it? You'll have to stop on your way north and get a cap someplace."

"I should've checked his work before I left the place. But I didn't, so it's my own fault."

"It's not a big deal, except you'll have to find a place to get another one. As long as you keep your black and gray water valves closed, you'll be OK. We can ask at the office. There might be an RV repair shop on the island. Seems it's always something with these RV's, isn't it? Did you know that you get cable with the lot?"

"Really!"

To say the least I was anxious to try it. After a half hour of plugging and twisting, Liz and I decided the cable box on the camper hadn't been connected. There wouldn't be any television for this little gal. We were as remote as one could get without leaving the country. I wasn't too disgruntled because it opened the door for an invitation to dinner in Liz and Bruce's motor home. At six o'clock I knocked on their door.

Liz called out, "Come on in."

The climb into the big rig ended in a spectacular view of their coach. Three slide-outs on the wide body, Class-A camper made it very comfortable. The smell of leather lingered. Mirrors reflected the crystal goblets, the silver, the china and the serving dishes on the set table. We dined, gabbed for hours about owning hotels and going deep sea fishing. In that brief time we became friends.

A couple of days later Liz asked if I'd like to go into Key West. I accepted even though my body ached from hiking the day before. This time I'd take my putter and use it like a cane. After Liz had parked her jeep on a side street, I grabbed the hand bar on the ceiling, and slid to the pavement. The next thing in my hand was the putter.

"Say…that putter would make a handy weapon, wouldn't it?" Liz said.

I looked from the putter to her and chuckled, "I hadn't thought about that, but I guess it would."

"Don't worry! I've got us covered," she said as she patted her handbag. "I have a pistol in my purse."

Amazed, but not concerned, I continued to walk down the street with my pistol packing mama. We proceeded toward the docks to see the ships, the seaside entertainment, and the boardwalk that was peppered with unusual shops.

Our first discovery led us to a specialty shop full of crazy hats. Liz grabbed one after another, posing for the camera with her favorite, the Mad Hatter. An ice cream parlor next door begged us to enter. We ordered our favorite cones at six dollars each and retired to a bench in the blazing sun. Giggling and slurping, we licked the sides of the cone to keep up with its melting rivers.

As we walked, my awareness turned to individuals pushing grocery baskets full of junk. The homeless seemed to be everywhere, some asleep in corners, some on benches. One young man, I guessed in his twenties, was propped against the wrought iron fence of the Hilton Hotel. His clothes were tattered and dirty. He lay like a puppet, as though he had been dropped that way. A pyramid of unkempt, blonde hair crossed his face, ending at his shoulders. I watched him to see if he was breathing. Looking up, I saw a man seated inside the hotel's fence, selling tickets for events.

"Sir, I'm concerned about this young man. He doesn't seem to be…"

He frowned as he interrupted me, "Oh, he's just drunk—step over him. These guys are all over the place down here."

Liz touched my elbow, guiding me away. "Pretty sad, isn't it? They come down here for the winter because it's the warmest place they can find. Remember what Christ said, the poor are always with us. It's just more blatant here."

As we proceeded through town, we came upon more and more young people who made their homes on the streets. I pretended that everything was right with the world, that there weren't people who couldn't afford a fabulous meal like Liz and I had shared.

By the time we arrived at the docks, hundreds of people had gathered, hoping to see a spectacular sunset.

As the sun began to touch the horizon, a cruise ship parked in front of our view. People complained. Someone said, "Maybe it'll move," but it didn't. The sun's flaming mass hidden by the ship cast rays that couldn't be contained. Brilliant shades escaped from its sides as they speared across the darkening waters. I stood amongst a crowd of people whose only concern was to be favored with a beautiful sunset, not the reality that surrounded them. Their favor hid in a shadow like the blatant presence of the poor who had no place to lay their heads.

On our way back to the jeep, we lingered for a few moments at some shops. Liz surprised me with a remembrance gift. The words "my best friend" were inscribed on the front of the cotton T-shirt. I tried to be excited about it, but my heart was heavy from the weariness seen that day.

Later as I lay in bed, I asked a special blessing for my new friend and thanked my heavenly Father for all the blessings I had been given. I envisioned the scenes that had repeated themselves in town. I tried to realize the hardships the homeless must endure, but knew I couldn't.

Was there one prayer that could cover all the despair?

My spirit answered, and I was prompted to recite the Our Father, dedicating it to those who didn't know how to pray.

Chapter 25

Few campers knew about Aqua Isles in Labelle because it had nestled a block off the main street and marked only by a faded sign. David and I had spent a month there, so I knew some folks in the campground. The meridian off the main avenue of the park was dappled with tall pines and palm trees that led the way to the Caloosahatchee riverfront. Benches and swings were placed sporadically across the lawn to entice the seniors to relax and watch the boats go by. I decided to stay for a month.

The Christmas decorations seemed out of place without snow. A Santa balanced on a steel rod in front of a motor home, palm trees were entwined with lights, and oversized ornaments caught the sunlight as they peeked from the branches of the evergreens.

As I drove to my space, men came from all directions. Seeing a mature female driving a big motor home must've been a treat for the male aptness.

One of the fellows shouted, "Don't worry about a thing, ma'am. We'll get you back into that space with no trouble at all."

Within minutes, several fellows began shouting orders.

"Turn the wheel to the left," one guy yelled.

"Turn the wheel to the right," another guy hollered.

The steering wheel swiveled back and forth to their commands. Although I appreciated the help, I got frustrated trying to follow all the orders.

As men's nature was to direct and women tend to do as they are told, I became exasperated with their overly zealous approach. Finally, I stuck my head out of the window and shouted, "I can't do both things at once!"

A man waved his hand in disgust, grumbling as he walked away, "Too many bosses."

Twenty minutes later the coach sat in its space, well—sort of. Unsure of where I had actually ended up with all the coaching, I got out of the camper. The ledge of the concrete patio hugged my back tire and the entry door was over the grass. I groaned when I saw the scrape marks on the side of the tire.

Between Nickie's place and here this coach is going to start looking like it got in a battle with a wild cat.

The man standing next to me said, "That won't make no difference on those tires."

Being a wee bit upset, I thanked him and excused myself. I would wait until the guys disappeared into their own worlds. Then I'd pull the coach out and realign it with the patio. Since the tires rested in grooves, the bottom of the coach was too close to the ground. With the lessons I got in Venice, I knew the jacks wouldn't clear. Unfortunately, I didn't have enough boards to raise the coach. The solution would demand more digging. At least this time the coach would stay put for a month.

One thing I didn't have, nor did I think I'd ever need, was a shovel. I decided to walk down the road and ask the first man that I saw for one. A block away I spotted a tall slender fellow with snow-white hair inside of his workshop. I remembered him from the last time David and I stayed in the park. When he saw me he waved, sending a broad smile and a happy hello. It was just the invitation I needed.

Extending my hand in a greeting, I said, "Good afternoon. I just arrived in the park."

"I'm pleased to meet you," he said. "My name is Pat. I'm not Irish, although I've been told that I'm full of the blarney."

"With that smile I'm not surprised. I don't know if you remember me. David and I were here a few years back."

"Sure I do, I always remember a troublemaker."

"Haven't changed a bit, have you, Pat."

"Oh, I try to keep people guessing. So what can I do for you?"

I explained the situation with my jacks and asked if he had a hoe or a shovel, anything that I could dig with.

"As a matter of fact I do."

He walked toward the storage shed that had been converted into his workshop. When he came back he held a small shovel, maybe three feet long. The edges shone silver as though it had been polished by the earth. With gentleness Pat told me about its history, digging trenches during WW11.

Having had three brothers in that war, it wasn't difficult to get involved in his story.

As he handed me the shovel, I told him I'd take good care of it.

He laughed to the bottom of his socks, "You can't do anything to that shovel that hasn't been done already."

Sentiment filled my eyes. I thanked him for letting me take it. Walking back to the camper, its history brought memories of air raid drills and visions of nuns and children running down basement stairs, fearing that this time there would be real bombs.

Being sandwiched between two park models, gave me a neighbor on either side. To the north of my camper was a younger couple who stayed to themselves. However, the other neighbor had no trouble using up their time. Chester, an eighty-six year old gentleman with a severe hearing loss, had no intention of wearing his hearing aids. As a result, his television entertained everyone within earshot on the nights that he couldn't sleep.

Chester had lost his wife about five years prior. The campground gossip affirmed that he hadn't found a reason to adjust to the loss of his longtime mate, until he discovered I was a widow. Daily, he made trips to my side door, wooing me with homemade blueberry muffins.

"You can be confident I have a clean kitchen," he said.

That made me wonder if it were true. Nevertheless, I returned his kindness with polite conversation. However, his inappropriate responses revealed he didn't understand a word that had been said, but that didn't stop his pursuit.

When he realized I didn't have a car, he tempted me with an offer. "I'd be pleased to drive you into Ft. Myers or to the store if need be to get a few things. I go to Ft. Myers often. It wouldn't be an inconvenience."

I declined his kind offer. The thought of driving in a car with a man who refused to wear his hearing aids made me uncomfortable.

The next day I mentioned Chester's offer to Pat. "Oh no! Don't want to do that. Chester just about got himself killed a couple of times this last month. He's been driving in and out of some pretty deep ditches, and not on purpose."

Well, so much for a free ride to the store. After that I did my best to avoid him as nicely as possible. It seemed like the only way to save both of our lives.

Since my arrival the days had been warm, so I decided to put down the awning. I had called the company who made it for instructions. After going over the information, I wondered why I bothered. The drawings were very technical. The smart thing to do would be to ask for some help. I walked down to Betty and Pat's home to see if they knew anyone for the job.

Betty, who was a tall, medium-framed lady with silver-gray hair, and more than likely five years my senior, had a smile that sparkled in her eyes like Christmas lights.

When I rapped on their door, I saw Pat gesture for me to come in.

Seeing Betty, I said, "Hi, Betty! I don't know if you remember me. David and I were parked next to you and Pat about four years ago. I bought a motor home and I'm parked at the end of the street. In fact, Pat just gave me his army shovel to use."
"Sure I do. You bought a motor home? Where's David?"
"I'm sorry to say that David died last summer from a rare form of Lou Gehrig's disease."
"Oh, that's terrible. Who are you traveling with now?"
"No one...I travel alone."
"Seriously?"
"Afraid so. I decided life is too short to sit around, feeling sorry for myself. I've always wanted to see the country, so that's what I plan to do. When we traveled, David never liked to stop. He just kept going and going and going. I often got a kink in my neck from trying to see what I had missed."
"Well, I must say you have more courage than I do. You're one gutsy lady."
"Never thought of it like that before. Sometimes I think I'm crazy because I get myself in a fair amount of jams, but I keep going. By the way, do you happen to know anyone who would be willing to help me put my awning down? I'm afraid to try it by myself."
"You bet. We have a fellow in the park from Canada who helps everybody with repairs and

such. He lives right across on K Street in that Pace Arrow. His name is Zollie. He really knows his stuff."

I thanked her for the name. It would be refreshing to know somebody who knew "his stuff" for a change.

The Pace Arrow parked across the street had seen better days. The faded tan exterior dated it by twelve to fifteen years. An old oak tree hovered high above the camper, protecting it from the glaring sun that mercilessly dried out rubber roofs. A small stool had been placed beneath the lowest step of the motor home to accommodate an entry. I reached up and rapped on the bottom of the door. A fellow, with white hair jutting from under a small, blue fishing hat, hooks in place, answered. Other than his clothes, I thought I had just met Santa Claus, rosy cheeks and all.

"What can I do for you, young lady?" he asked with a warm smile.

"I was told that you were real handy with things and wondered if you'd help me. I'd like to put my awning down. I have zero experience with an awning."

Tipping his hat he said, "And when do you want to do this?"

"Whenever it's convenient for you."

"How about if I come by in the morning, say about nine. Does that work for you?"

"That would be great. I'll see you in the morning."

First thing in the morning I got the tool for the awning out of the back bin. I put it on the picnic table along with paper and pencil to write Zollie's instructions. Seems my short term memory got a clean slate as soon as the words arrived. I had to make sure I had good notes. I didn't want to embarrass myself by having to ask him again.

Zollie arrived on time and went right to work. He walked from one side of the awning to the other, loosening knobs and pulling levers. It was like watching Sally the day I bought the RV. The awning went down so fast, I didn't know it happened. I wrote as fast as I could, but that didn't do the job.

"You don't have to write, just watch."

"I'm afraid I'll forget a step and jam something."

Smiling broadly he chuckled, "It's a very simple process made up of <u>four easy steps</u>. The people who built these awnings did so with the understanding that seniors would be handling them. As a result, the awning comes down and goes back up with these <u>four easy to remember steps.</u> You won't forget."

Past panic over motor home problems reminded me that I'd forget. I did my best to listen to every word; however, he went through the steps so fast, turning his head away as he spoke. So I picked up very little of the instructions.

"I'm sorry, Zollie. I should've told you. I have a severe hearing loss. I'm only getting bits and pieces of what you are saying."

"That's OK. I'll tell you again when I get done, just watch. There's one thing that I don't want you to ever forget. When you put the awning back in its housing, don't ever wrap your hand around the awning bar to get it to go in next to the coach. Always use a flat hand and push on the outside of the bar. If you grab the bar instead of using a flat hand, the bar can go in so fast it'll snap your fingers right off."

Anything he had managed to teach me up to that point, vanished. Not letting go of the cord seemed a minor dilemma next to this piece of information. I wondered if I'd always be afraid of the awning.

Looking at a face that must've had panic written across it, Zollie said, "Don't worry. It's only a simple four step procedure."

Simple procedure! I've heard that one before. Things are always easy when you know how to do them. It's when you're a neophyte that you get into trouble. I'll have to write the instructions later.

The next day, I took my full page version of the "simple four step procedure" over to Zollie to approve. The motivation for this act was definitely being scared of losing a friendly member of my body.

With the awning down I could finally begin to relax in its shade. It helped block the sun's rays, providing relief for me and the refrigerator.

The days continued to be warm, especially for the middle of January. This particular afternoon the temperature reached into the high seventies. Feeling like summer, I decided to put on a pair of shorts and a little jersey top. The weatherman predicted a warm, calm day. He didn't mention any signs of high winds or rain. The awning shouldn't be a problem. Of course, the forecast can be as unpredictable as the weather. David had lost two awnings, thinking the weather wouldn't change. The first one had been with a sudden gust of wind; the other was ripped from the camper by a heavy rain storm. Neither awning had been anchored to the ground or tilted for drainage. Looking around at other coaches, my straps and two metal pieces that screwed into the ground to stabilize the awning had been left behind.

By the time five o'clock rolled around, the wind began to change. A nip in the air convinced me to put the awning up. I looked over the instructions, confident that I could do the job. After all, there were only four simple steps to this procedure. All I had to do was reverse the process. It couldn't be that hard.

First, I loosened the black knobs on the sidebars.

Climbing up the step ladder, Zollie's words echoed in my head, *If you have to get on a ladder, you're probably doing something wrong.*

I rationalized that he was much taller than I. After that, I threaded the black nylon cord and pushed it over to the arrow in the center of the awning bar, hanging on tight. A chilling wind passed as I questioned whether or not I had forgotten anything. I reached into the pocket of my shorts. The instructions weren't there. I glanced toward the motor home. The instructions were laying on the step inside the coach, out of my reach unless I let go of the cord. I tried to stay calm and consider the situation. Then I noticed the lock housed on the sidebar.

That has to be the next step.

The awning had to be released to go up. The cord slid through the slot, following me toward the lock. I strained to reach up to release the lock. The awning began to move upward, entwining the cord.

I yanked the cord to stop the ascending awning. My heart rate went from sixty to a hundred and sixty as the pulsations banged in my temples. I tugged on the cord. I couldn't bring it back down. I had been captured by the cord, shivering in my summer clothes.

I'll have to get help from somebody, but there isn't a soul on the street.

There's always somebody out riding a bike or walking. Where are they all? Typical...when you need help there's no one around.

I began to pray that someone would come along. Did I hear God say, "Not you again!" Fifteen minutes passed, then twenty. Dusk was ending the day with a breeze that sent a chilly reminder of winter. I envisioned a frozen statue hanging on to an awning cord as I made St. Peter's acquaintance. Just before eternity arrived, a figure approached on a three-wheel tricycle. I hollered and waved with my free hand to get the person's attention. A lady in her eighties hobbled over to my side. I explained my stupidity and asked her to find Zollie.

In her exuberance, she left the tricycle sitting in the road and ran down the street screaming, "HELP."

I saw Zollie approaching. He didn't say a word and he wasn't smiling. I went to relinquish the cord into his care, but he rejected it.

"Don't let go of that," he warned.

"Never," I whimpered.

Walking back and forth from one end of the awning to the other, he tugged on the bar until I thought it would snap. After much effort, he got the bar extended and the awning back into its housing.

Not smiling, he reminded me, "You forgot to put the side arms down. Remember, there are only <u>four simple steps</u>. You forgot the second one. I'll be over in the morning and you can practice putting the awning up and down until you're comfortable with it. In the meantime, study the instructions you wrote down."

With total humiliation, I thanked him and retreated into the coach, never wanting to be seen again. It was an embarrassing way to learn that instructions inside the coach are hard to read from outside the coach. One would think that the fading sunlight would've been a clue on a January evening. The stupid part of my brain now had a storehouse full of hindsight.

Chapter 26

After a month of being dependent on others to get my weekly groceries, I wanted to leave Aqua Isles. My daughter said I'd go crazy without a car. However, with all that had happened, I didn't need a car on the back of the camper to complicate matters. Somehow, I'd have to overcome my fear of towing a vehicle or stay cooped up in an RV park where I knew few people. My bike had saved my sanity somewhat, allowing a trip to the library for email and to pick up a couple of staples. But the freedom to cruise the area, find special places of interest, or make a trip into Ft. Myers was nonexistent. Of course, I could've always cruised the ditches with Chester, my eighty-year old neighbor.

I had no idea where to go next. There hadn't been a need for an agenda because I had made arrangement to stay in Venice all winter. Heading north the end of February would be precarious as far as road conditions are concerned and too much of a temperature change for my body. Campground fees, by the night or the week, would be expensive, but living in WalMart lots or Flying J's truck stops for a month wouldn't work either. Looking at the atlas, the Florida Panhandle seemed like a good place to explore. I knew some folks in Pensacola, so it would be more than just a scenic drive.

First I needed to replace the missing sewer cap. I headed inland to Conicare, an RV service center in the middle of the state.

A tall, elderly gentleman extended his hand in a welcome.

"What can we do for you, Missy?"

"Well, sir..."

"Call me, Jim."

With such a congenial fellow, I decided to shared my story about the electric valve. Jim knelt down on the gravel roadway with ease to check my valve.

Shaking his head, "We hate to see this sort of thing happen. It gives the rest of us a bad reputation. That manual valve they told you they didn't have? Well, it's a standard piece of equipment. It fits almost all RV's and it's very unusual for a dealer not to have one in stock. I think you got took, Missy. They stuck you with a three hundred dollar electric valve when the manual one costs about twenty bucks."

Angry and still shaking his head, Jim walked into the store with me right behind him. He grabbed a cap and handed it to me. "Never mind," he said as he pulled his hand back, "I'll put it on for you. At least you'll get your money's worth here."

During the installation, which took him less than a minute, Jim talked to me about the drive along highway 98. "It's the way Florida used to be. Best to avoid Interstate 10; it's pretty rough."

I agreed. David and I traveled Interstate 10 with the thirty-eight foot Mountain Aire on our way to New Orleans. It was like a tugboat pulling a cruise ship on the high seas—one going up with the one going down. After about a hundred miles of this, David decided to try a different road. So he headed south to pick up a western route without checking the map. Hmm. Suddenly, we were face to face with the ocean and no way to turn around.

David said, "It'll be a challenge, but I can get it done."

With a grumpy look, he pointed to where I should stand to give directions. He made sure I understood that the job would be tough enough without me standing in the wrong place. I could feel the disaster about to happen, like a train coming at me with a full head of steam.

He screamed.

I moved.

"How do you think I can see you if you can't see me," he yelled.

Was that a rhetorical statement? I finally figured out that if I could see myself in the side mirrors, he had to be able to see me. He didn't scream so I assumed he could.

A good chunk of the day went into his chosen detour, but David didn't give up. He tried another road, again without looking at a map. Bound for Mobile, Alabama, this side trip took us over miles of narrow, steel guarded bridges. I prayed that the trucks wouldn't come, but they did—and they wanted their half of the road. Nothing slow them down either. David challenged them head on. I couldn't take it. I ducked as they approached and I don't know why. This tactic wouldn't keep me from being smashed. Terror wouldn't either.

I thanked Jim for the scenic route and his help. The news on the valve didn't come as a surprise. It reminded me that being alone, I'd be seen as an easy target. This was the first time I had been taken, shame on them, unless you count my perfect spot. The next time it won't be so easy.

As soon as I veered off Interstate 75 to pick up 98 the temperature began to change. I should've realized I'd be facing cooler temperatures, but who thinks of freezing when you're enjoying the eighty degree temperatures of southern Florida? Being on my adventure, I didn't have to consider anything other than earthquakes, tornadoes, and maybe flash floods. If my carefree attitude got bathed in the cold, damp weather of the Panhandle, too bad, a gulf view would be worth it. After a couple hundred miles of shivering, my tune changed along with my clothing. My garb went from shorts to sweats and a jacket. For sure, I wouldn't be dry camping. I needed a nice cozy campground.

Highway 98 presented with a shaded pathway that weaved toward the gulf and then darted back under the cover of the trees. A mixture of undergrowth entwined the palms and evergreens that towered over beds of white wild flowers.

When glistening waters emerged, I stopped and sat for an hour or two on the beach, feeding the sea gulls. White foam touched the shore with a soothing rhythm as I listened to the surf. With a deep breath, my lungs opened to the fresh sea air. The sand felt cool under my feet, the breeze gentle, the time peaceful.

David sure had a thing about me towing those fifth wheels. I don't know who he thought would drive if he had a heart attack. I remember the

145

time he was choking so hard that he started to turn blue. I begged him to pull over, but no. He didn't stop when I screamed at him either. Strange! He stopped choking though. And here I am driving a motor home. This would give him fits.

Before I returned to the camper, I picked up the newspaper to read the funnies. The real world caught my eye. It was March 18, 2003. The headlines announced a bombing in Iraq. Machine guns and rockets were finding their targets in that part of the world. A plane had crashed; all were killed. Parents hoped that it was someone else's son or daughter. Others were protecting our country so I could enjoy these moments on the shore. With a wounded heart, I walked back to the motor home and continued my journey.

By the time I reached Biloxi, the gulf was displaying its beauty, widespread and distant. It would be a good place to spend some time. I imagined long walks and the fresh smell of the sea. The campground hid a half block behind the tree lined road that ran along the ocean. I could ride my bike for miles. This would be my haven.

Dream on, Macbeth! Enjoying my fantasy, I paid for a week, never noticing the train tracks until I parked the camper. They were no more than a hundred feet in front of my campsite, and they ran the entire length of the park. Moving to another spot wouldn't accomplish a thing.

No, the owner wouldn't refund my money, but I could leave. Being frugal or better yet—feeling taken again, I had no intention of paying for the lot and ending up with nothing. Besides, it was rare that I could hear much after I took my hearing aids out. I'd probably sleep right through any racket just like a baby.

Just before bedtime, the first train performed its whistle or shall I say blast. My peace and quiet had encountered a noisy death. Just about the time I had begun to relax, another shrill whistle pierced the humid night air, long and hard. I tried everything, even covering my head with my pillow, but nothing helped. Crossroads were plentiful. The only relief came as the train distanced itself from the campground. I conceded to exhaustion and passed out around three in the morning. After a week of that, I knew the train-line had hired every neurotic power-crazed engineer they could find. I left without a twinge of regret. I loved being close to the water, but not enough to tolerate more whistles.

I looked for a different park, only to find the same situation. The tracks ran behind every park in the area. For the life of me I couldn't understand why anyone would want to visit this insanity. Then it dawned on me, the casinos. The invitation was clear: park your rig free while you spend your dollars. I heard there were plenty of rigs cashing in on that free parking. Did I say free?

Most of the casinos were close to or on the ocean and a good distance from the train whistles. That sounded pretty good to me.

The casino lot was spotted with oil, black wads of gum and plenty of trash. I weaved my way through several coaches, looking for another perfect spot. Finding none I settled for the least slanted piece of pavement. I got somewhat edgy after a few nights. There were too many people from all walks of life parked too close. Some were too happy and some were not happy at all. The next morning I left the winners and losers behind and drove north to the nearest WalMart.

My atlas showed a superstore far from the tracks. As I set up camp, the security guard made his rounds for the evening. I tried my jacks, but they hadn't changed their disposition. They performed exactly like they did before they were supposedly, "functioning according to their design." Ho hum! Determined that they were going to work right, I decided to call the dealership in the morning. After supper I'd go for a walk and maybe visit a camper or two.

An all-American gal with a sheen to her skin and a look I thought went out of fashion years ago, answered the door I knocked on. Not for a second did I feel like I had intruded upon Jane's time. Her attitude sparkled and her voice rang clear with a joyous tone. Learning that she and her husband were traveling missionaries, I knew her glow came from deep inside. Exuberant about her faith, she gave me little brochures filled with prayers that were gentle reminders of the Father that watches over us.

Behind her I could see a young girl sitting on the sofa. A computer game lay next to her, no longer a challenge against her wit. Jamie, a petite seven-year-old, seemed very bored. Seeing I had been observing the child, Jane introduced me. My suspicions were confirmed when Jamie said that looking at scenery had become an endless line of trees and bushes. She wanted to go home. Jamie's parents meant for the trip to add another dimension to her life. She would learn about serving God and caring for others as the family went forth with their "Walk for Him" ministry. My heart peaceful, I went back to the camper, ready for sweet dreams.

Early the next morning I called the dealership. They authorized the repair and gave me the name of an RV service center in Biloxi where I could get the work done. Upon arriving for my appointment, I told the service manager that I had already gotten authorization.

He called Richmond to confirm, but whoever answered the phone refused authorization. I insisted that he try again. Being unsuccessful the second time, the technician tried to convince me with fear tactics to have the repairs done. What if I couldn't get the jacks to come down, or worse yet, back up! The repair would be around seven hundred dollars. The good news was that I wouldn't have to pay the hundred dollars for the diagnostic, if they did the repairs.

This should pacify me?

By the time he finished his pitch, I was no longer a happy camper. The big man routine against the little woman hadn't worked. Now familiar with a snow job, I reversed the roles to "big woman against little man."

Not wanting to deal with a wild woman, he decided to put the fire out by taking a look at the jacks. Like everyone else, he pushed the arrows on the control panel, making the coach do its little dance. Then he crawled under the coach.

After several minutes I heard, "They're working the way they're designed to work."

Not again!

"But they are hanging up and coming down too fast," I argued. "Nobody could get a chock under the pads."

Ignoring the chock part of my sentence, "Oh, I wouldn't worry about that," he said as he crawled out from under the unit. "Some jacks are just temperamental, a quirk. . . you know."

No! I don't know. They are not functioning the way they were designed. I read the blasted manual!

"I suggest you take it back to the folks you bought it from if you're not happy."

Hearing that statement I figured he didn't want to deal with this lady any longer. Considering the contradiction of "a repair of seven hundred dollars" compared to "the jacks are functioning according to design," I didn't want to deal with him either. I'd have to reroute my trip home to include a stop in Richmond, Indiana. The dealership should be accountable for the jacks. The technician was one hundred percent correct on that note. In the meantime, I intended to enjoy the trip west along the ocean until I reached Baton Rouge. There I'd begin my drive north.

I had little opportunity to use the generator because I had been plugged into thirty amp service

over the winter. Staying parked at truck stops or
WalMart changed this routine.

As eight o'clock had arrived, I could turn on
the generator without disturbing anyone. In order to
hear the generator start, I opened the window over
the dinette, tuned my hearing aids to loud and
pushed the starter on the control panel. Nothing
happened. At first I thought my hearing aid battery
had died. I spoke to test it, but it was fine. I turned
back to the control panel to check the level for the
coach batteries. Nothing lit up. My batteries were
dead. I slumped down on the sofa to prepare myself
for a panic attack.

*What could possibly be wrong this time? I
guess there won't be any toast for breakfast.*

Not knowing the area, I went back to my
neighbors. They told me there was an Auto Zone
about a half mile down the road. They tested
batteries for free to see if there were any dead cells.
With a thank you, I was on my way.

Dan, at Auto Zone, a dark-haired, heavyset
man in his thirties, checked the batteries. Getting
down on all fours, he went right to work, making
connections. While he took care of his job, I paged
through the manual to see what kind of batteries I
would need, just in case. The batteries were dead
and bone-dry. Although Dan never said it, I knew it
was my fault.

The technician in Richmond told me the
batteries only needed to be checked every six
months. So I didn't realize I needed to check them.
Dan said in the warm weather they should be
checked at least once a month. As I didn't want

another expensive lesson, I quizzed Dan on the type
of batteries he planned to install. He held his
patience, showing me what was printed on the
outside. When he finished the job, I went back to
WalMart.

Now that I had two brand new batteries, I
could use the generator for dinner. Toast—here I
come. I completed the same routine as before and
pushed the starter.

The coach began to vibrate violently.

Now what?

My hearing aids were picking up the sound
from all directions. I couldn't determine the source.
My feet told me the rumble seemed mostly in the
floor. I began to feel my way from the kitchen
toward the cab.

I imagined that something drastic might
happen, like the camper blowing up. I had to solve
the problem fast. By the time I reached the front of
the camper, I knew the vibrations were coming
from below the swivel chair, right above the new
batteries. I ran to the stove and turned off the
generator.

*The batteries must have been connected
wrong. David would know what to do. I guess I'll
have to go back to Auto Zone in the morning to find
out what's wrong.*

It would be another cool night without a
furnace. I wasn't giving the batteries a second
chance.

I arrived at Auto Zone a little before eight.
Shortly afterwards, Dan arrived. A puzzled look
crossed his face as he glanced my way.

At eight o'clock sharp, I went into the store to find Dan. I told him about the problem. He went right to the motor home, pulled out the battery tray and checked all the connections.

"The connections are fine. I don't know what the problem is, ma'am."

Dan got his boss and he checked the connections. He found everything in order. I asked Dan if I should turn on the generator, so he could see what happened.

"Yeah! That'll help."

The coach began to vibrate. Dan followed the vibration, working his way inside the coach and toward the chair. Reaching under it, he found the culprit. I stared in amazement at my vibrator.

Grinning, Dan said, "Here's your problem, ma'am. Turning the generator on must have shook the vibrator enough to start it. Sure enough, it's been slammed against the metal plate on the bottom of the chair."

The generator purred as sweet as a kitten once the vibrator had been removed. As embarrassing as the moment was, I had to laugh. "I am so sorry to have caused all this trouble."

Dan joined me in laughter, "No bother. Glad we could help. Besides, it'll make for some interesting conversation for the rest of the day. It's not often that we have a story like this to tell."

Chapter 27

The clear skies of winter were evident on the way to Baton Rouge. Bridges climbed high, giving the illusion that one would plunge to the water at the top. A couple from Biloxi said the sights in Baton Rouge deserved a day or two for exploration.

The pungent smell of paper mills filled the air as I entered town. Chuckholes, too many to dodge, hollowed the uneven blacktop, keeping my speed at twenty miles per hour. Even at that, dishes bounced in the cupboards, cabinets popped open, and the small garbage pail rolled back and forth across the hallway. It was a Lucille Ball comedy, only there weren't any rocks hidden in the camper.

By the time I reached the north side of town, my attitude had gone from the sight-seeing mode to the forward mode. Natchez would have to provide my entertainment until I headed toward the northern winds.

A WalMart, not far from the Mississippi river, would be my home base as I toured the city. The pleasant weather and the history of the town had enticed me to stay for a few days. Then I'd go to St. Charles, stopping to see my brother for a week or two.

The security guard at WalMart told me I could park toward the back of the store. As I drove around to the back, I noticed that the decibels coming off the store's cooling system were high enough to cause a hearing loss. High power lines edged the border of the lot, humming their presence. Several fifth wheels and trailers had parked in the level section under the wires, leaving no room for a newcomer. I'd have to park in the slanted middle area. That was OK. I felt safer with the others there, regardless of the slant.

I made a couple of attempts to level the coach, but the jacks couldn't clear the pavement. Since I had enough boards to bring up the slanted side, I used them for the job. Then I hauled out my lounge chair. Its sagging seat and uneven stance told the story of overuse by a much heavier person.

After reading for a half hour my stomach growled. Dinner time had arrived so I needed to start the generator. A push of a button and the digits on the microwave lit up and the refrigerator switched from gas to electric. Just as readily, I had a knock on the side door. I called out, asking who it was, and heard a mumbled response.

I shouted, "Whoever you are, go to the cab window so I can see you."

I wasn't about to open the door to a stranger in a isolated WalMart parking lot.

Getting to the passenger's window, a man with a scowl on his face stared back at me.

"How long are you going to run that thing," he screamed over the noise pollution from the store. "You're stinking up the whole place."

I almost laughed. *This is a WalMart parking lot, not the Ritz.*

Deep creases across his brow and between his eyes sketched the anger he voiced.

This guy is one unhappy dude and not just tonight. I'm sure he thinks he can bully me.

I had been in and out of the unit several
times so he knew I didn't have a man around to
punch him in the nose.

I stuck my nose in the air and said, "I'm
making my dinner and it'll run as long as I need it
to, at least an hour, maybe longer."

I turned and walked back to the kitchen,
deciding to do exactly that. Of all the people I had
met, he held the stinker award. I planned to wipe
him out of my memory bank and concentrate on the
nice folks, like the fellows who spent time teaching
me about motor homes and the mechanic in Florida
who crawled under the coach just to check my
transmission fluid for the jacks. One turkey in a
group of eagles wouldn't spoil my day.

It had been a few days since I had checked
my email. I could do it at the library and they're
usually downtown. So I ventured forth. Meandering
through the streets, I ended up on a narrow road in a
residential area.

Oh brother, I've got myself in another jam.
Maybe I can find somebody to get me back on track.

As I drove, I spotted a gentleman hurrying
to put some things into his trunk. I called to him,

"Sir, I do believe I'm lost. I'm looking for
the library, but I got caught on these streets that
wind and twine in every direction. Can you help
me?"

He laughed as he glanced at the size of the
motor home. "I believe you are. I'm almost finished
loading the car, so if you have a minute, I'll lead
you right over there."

He led me through the maze of streets to where I could park the camper. Safely parked, the man came to the coach and gave me directions to the library.

"You have a good day now," he said.

I grabbed his hand with both of mine, thanking him for his guidance, another eagle.

Right across the street from the library, gardeners primped the colorful landscaping of a historical mansion. A wraparound porch accented by a hand carved railing, etched glass in a solid maple door, and bric-a-brac trim reached to the peaks of the three-story home. This magnificent memory would stay with me for a long time.

After checking my email, I spoke to the librarian. When she learned of my route to St. Louis, she said, "You're in for a treat. If you haven't been this way before and you enjoy scenery, you have to drive the Natchez Trace Parkway. It's a diagonal road so it would be a more logical choice for your trip to St. Louis anyway."

I decided to follow her advice, turning onto the Parkway the next day.

An ancient riverbed turned west toward the Mississippi through eloquent pines. The sun weaved its way in and out of the trees as it flashed its light against the narrow roadway. Like the ocean, I stopped at the waysides. I took my time to enjoy the beauty of the Losee Bluff, to sit on a cool boulder under the shrouded sky. Peace reigned in God's holy presence.

On my first stop after the Parkway, I learned that my brother Tom had had emergency surgery for an aortic aneurysm. By the time I arrived at the hospital, they were going to send him home the next day. *Things sure have changed. Major surgery one day, ICU the next two and out you go.*

A large parking lot butted up against Tom's apartment building. Management allowed me to park in the lot so I could help with his care. I stayed until he could manage with the help of Home Health Care, and long enough to pick up some nasty germs from his grandchildren.

With a stuffy head, I drove the rig onto Interstate 70 a couple of weeks later. It would take me all the way to Richmond, Indiana. Being sick, I grumbled a litany of should've. I wanted to be going home but couldn't because the tech had put a seal over mildew. No one else had been on the roof. It would be interesting to hear their side of the story. The jacks, my favorite pain in the nervous system, were still not functioning according to the manual. My honey had turned to vinegar. Now I wanted the jacks fixed and the seals rechecked, and they could pay to have my ceiling cleaned from the leak.

At my first stop, I called the dealership in Richmond to get an appointment. To my surprise, a gal had replaced Ben, the service manager. I explained the situation with the jacks and the leaky ceiling as pleasantly as I could after a winter full of nightmares. Jamie said she'd check into it. At this point I can't say I believed her, but I tried.

"Could you please call me in a couple of days when you know when you'll be arriving? That's the only way I can schedule your appointment," she said.

Two days later, I called.

Getting Jamie on the phone, her words sent me into a tizzy.

"It seems somebody else thought there was something wrong with the jacks because they ordered parts. I'm sorry, but they were never installed. No wonder you were having trouble."

On the one side of the coin, I felt like jumping for joy. On the other, well, I'll leave that to the imagination. I sighed and went for "jump for joy." Thrilled that the problem had been solved, I opted to put all the grief and humiliation behind me. After the repairs I could drive home and start planning my trip to Washington State. I couldn't linger too long because I had received a letter from Esther (the lady who encouraged me to follow my dream), saying that her husband had died. Seeing the northwest coast had been a long awaited dream, this would be a good time to spend some time with her. The motor home could be parked next to her daughter's home. Esther lived a short walk from there. I prayed that it wasn't another perfect spot.

Before going to Washington state, I wanted to visit my family in Wisconsin. I planned to take Interstate 94, the northern route, stopping in Minnesota to have my hearing aids adjusted. My son, Greg, and the family were going to Glacier National Park, which meant they'd be taking the same road. If our schedules matched I'd have company part of the way. As they did, we'd meet on the western side of Minnesota. Greg warned that he didn't stop very often, only for food and gas. At that time the family tended to all their needs and took a good stretch. I wasn't sure that would work for me. I had already begun to slide into the easygoing life of a senior. Having a motor home, I could stop whenever nature called, but I was willing to give it a try.

I left Minneapolis to connect with Greg's family on the road after a brief visit with my niece and her family. By late morning, I noticed Greg's white Dodge Ram in the side view mirror. He was coming up fast. His truck, followed closely by their Gulf Stream camper, whizzed past. Everybody was waving, smiling and pointing. The ride of a lifetime was about to begin. My speedometer fluctuated between seventy-five on the downhill grade to fifty on the uphill grade, and there were plenty of those.

Maybe I would've been better off alone.

Often I had to pass Greg when climbing. I guessed my 450 had more gusto than his diesel truck. I'd never tell him that though.

My granddaughter decided to travel with me after the first stop, less crowded space and a front seat. Although I appreciated her company, keeping up a conversation and keeping up with Greg challenged my hearing and driving skills. By the time we had reached Billings, I gave them back their child. The ups and downs and the fast and slow pace had given me a good case of altitude sickness. It was time to settle in for the evening and let them go on their way. We said our goodbyes in a Burger King and I back tracked three miles to a Flying J's truck stop for the night. Tomorrow I'd continue at a much slower pace.

Chapter 28

By noon the heavens of the Big Sky Country were ablaze with a brilliant blue from the heat of the day. As I drove along Interstate 90, my carefree hairdo, which had taken its shape earlier that morning, had been straightened by the humidity and the wind. Giving up on the windows to provide comfort in the ninety degree temperature, I turned on the air. Although beautiful, the mountainous trip from Billings to Butte, Montana, topped at sixty-three-hundred and ninety feet as I crossed the Continental Divide. That climb took a fair amount of gas. I needed to conserve as much fuel as possible, especially if I'd have to run the generator to cool the coach.

I spotted an RV park off to my right as I drove by Deer Lodge, Montana. I thought about stopping because it looked rather barren with the sun melting the ground. Besides the day had just begun, and with the windows closed, the heat wasn't so bothersome. At breakfast I checked the road atlas for altitude and a good place to dry camp. I chose the WalMart in Missoula, as my destination. I'd be crossing another time zone as I headed west. I could easily make a couple hundred more miles. Then Bremerton, Washington, would be an easier drive.

A welcomed straight-a-way beyond Deer Lodge led me toward a beautiful mountainous backdrop of evergreens. The traffic was sparse, coming and going. A person would expect this in a state where the roads seem to go on forever. On rare occasions a truck would barrel past at better than seventy miles per hour, causing the motor home to sway from the gust of wind slapped against its side. The fellows at exercise class often talked about awnings and siding being ripped off of a coach with wild gusts of winds up to eighty mile an hour. When David and I went to California for my oldest brother's funeral, signs along the road warned of this possibility, but David kept right on going.

I believe in warnings, especially now. I felt very much alone, being accompanied only by the sound of the motor, the blowing of the air conditioner and miles of nothingness.

The sun continued its western journey, coming around to the driver's side. I reached for my sunglasses to cut the glare.

The sound of metal against metal vibrated through the coach, like an airplane sliding on its belly.

My hands tightened on the steering wheel.

My foot hit the brake, attempting to control the big rig.

Reaction enhanced thought. I checked my side mirrors immediately to see what I had hit as the RV began to respond. Billowy white particles filled the air behind the coach, like someone had opened a feather pillow.

With my heart pounding a number I didn't want to remember, I pulled to the side of the highway, turned off the motor and turned on my hazard lights. There I sat by MM 172 in the middle of nowhere with my hands shaking and with an uneven rhythm in my chest.

It didn't matter how I was feeling. I had to find out what had happened, and there wasn't anyone else for the job. As I slid out of the driver's seat, I looked east down the vacant road. Nothing was visible.

I must have hit something, but what?

Waves of heat penetrated my body as I walked around to the passenger's side of the coach. I prayed that the problem was something minor as I checked the front tires and the double rear tires on the passenger's side. My attention went to the back bin. It flapped open and closed with the wind.

Maybe something worked its way out of the bin and under the coach. But what was the feathery, white stuff, coming out of the backend?

I checked inside the bin. All the tools and gear were exactly where I had placed them.

Boy, the vibrations were bad enough to jolt the back bin open.

I secured the lock on the bin and sighed as I looked around to the rear of the coach. The bike was still on its rack. Not finding anything, my heart rate began to slow to its normal sixty beats per minute. I had convinced myself it had to be a fluke of some kind. I proceeded to the driver's side of the coach. The outside back tire looked OK, but for safety's sake I knew I had to check the inside tire as well.

Crouching down, I stared in astonishment at the wide strip of tread from the black, steel-belted radial. It lay almost completely peeled, leaving the tire naked and shriveled. My heart rate went back to its previous performance.

What am I going to do?

I didn't have a cell phone because I couldn't hear on one. The CB was useless, no signal anyway.

There wasn't a soul around and I could see for miles, both ways.

Maybe I can drive off the separation. I have three good tires in *the back. If I take it easy, I should be able to make the next town.*

I ran back to the cab, started the motor, and slowly pulled ahead. The tread remained captured by its keeper. My brilliant idea wasn't the smartest one I ever had. I doubted that I'd ever get anywhere, much less find a tire on a Saturday.

There have to be fifty or sixty miles between me and Missoula. WalMart would be open, but do they handle big enough tires for a motor home?

My next idea was more brilliant than trying to drive off an attached separation.

Turning off the motor, I went to the side of the highway and prayed, "Hey! I need some help down here."

An image of a pick-up truck passing a caravan became visible through the haze created by the heat. As the vehicles got closer, I could see that the caravan towed a travel trailer. I waved my arms back and forth, almost doing jumping jacks. The truck sped by, but the van pulled to the side of the road about fifty yards in front of the motor home. I stood amazed. Somebody had actually stopped.

A tall, slender young man, who I guessed was in his late thirties, came running toward me shouting, "What's the matter?"

164

Overwhelmed by my dilemma, tears filled my eyes.

"I have a flat on my inside back tire. I'm so glad you stopped."

"Are you OK?" he asked.

I wiped the tears from my cheeks and said, "I'm OK. I thank God for sending you to me."

He grinned. "I'm Steve. Don't worry, we'll see that you're taken care of. Do you have a cell phone by any chance?"

"No, I have a bad hearing loss. So far they haven't made one that I can hear on. I carry a CB, but there's no one to receive a signal out here. I do have road service though."

While I dug through my purse for the telephone number, Steve ran back to the caravan. He wanted to let his traveling companions know what had happened. I watched him until I realized I should thank the people in the caravan. I hurried after him.

Arriving at their van, I saw a handsome elderly gentleman behind the wheel, smiling softly. His cap shadowed his forehead, and his face was flushed from the heat. Behind him sat Grandma Jan, a pleasant-looking elderly lady whose face showed a wealth of embedded smile lines. Next to her sat Hilary, a bright-eyed, dark-haired young woman with a welcome smile as wide as her eyes. Two solemn boys with a younger girl between them were sitting behind them. This family of seven hailed all the way from Maine. They were on a once in a lifetime trip, exploring the northern portion of the country. I thanked them for stopping and Grandma

Jan said in a kindly manner, "That's OK. We're glad to be of help."

Grandpa Dave, the patriarch of the family, called road service and arranged for a tow truck while the youngest members waited in the Caravan. While Grandma Jan and Hilary, Steve's wife, gathered in conversation outside of the coach, I was busy being coached by the fellows as to what to do with the tire separation.

"We'll tie it up and put it in your back bin as soon as it's off the wheel," Steve said. "You'll need it when you go to the dealer on Monday morning. They'll want to check it for flaws. They won't even listen to you without it."

Hilary came to my side, holding a small booklet. "Here…we want you to have this. It's a small calendar with some thoughtful prayers."

I wondered if my eyes bespoke my gratitude. I thanked her, expecting the family to leave. However, they insisted on staying until road service arrived.

Squinting from the harsh sunlight, it dawned on me to invite the family into the camper. I received a mild decline to the invitation.

"You don't have to do that," Grandma Jan said.

A little gentle persuasion and they all conceded. I thought the younger generation might feel awkward going into a strange lady's motor home. Taking my teddy bears off the loveseat, I stacked them on the front shelves as though they were the welcoming committee. The youngsters watched as I arranged the bears, and I'm pretty sure

I heard a giggle or two. With the bears standing sentry, Tim, Heidi and Rob sat down on the loveseat.

Walking through the RV, I realized that the coach leaned toward the ditch. To relieve tension, I asked that everybody stay on the driver's side so we wouldn't roll down the hill. That broke the ice. Hilary suggested I open the blind at the back of the motor home, so we could see the tow truck coming.

The next thirty minutes were spent learning about the family's trip through Yellowstone and their planned travels to Washington State. On their way back to Maine, the final leg of their journey, they would go through the Canadian Rockies. As usual, I talked too much, sharing how I came to buy a motor home and be in the middle of nowhere.

"He's here!" someone shouted.

A jovial, middle aged man dressed in a one-piece gray work suit, hollered, "Howdy folks."

"This shouldn't be too bad," he said. "I won't even have to tow the motor home. I can fix it right where it sits."

Thank heavens. What a relief.

During his laborious task, a fringe of black hair lay around the nape of his neck, glistening in the sunlight. Perspiration beaded on his forehead and dripped from his chin, but he never complained. I offered him a cold drink a couple of times, but he declined.

With his Montana drawl he replied, "I'm just fine, ma'am. I do this stuff all the time."

As soon as the tire was off its rim, Grandpa Dave and Steve pulled the tread off. Then they wound it in a circle, tied it and put it in my back bin. Again, I expected the family to be on their way.

With a look of concern, Grandpa Dave approached. "We've decided that you should follow us into Missoula. You shouldn't be on the road without a spare. We know where the WalMart is and we can lead you right to it. We'll feel better once we know that you've been taken care of."

"That would be great."

"How fast do you drive?" he asked.

"Between fifty-five and sixty. I bet you must think I'm pretty stupid, traveling alone like this."

"No, on the contrary, I think you must be pretty smart or you never would've gotten this far."

Receiving this sincere compliment, my heart smiled.

"Ok, that sounds good," Grandpa Dave said. "We'll get going then. I'll be careful to watch in the side mirror, so we don't lose you."

After arriving at WalMart in Missoula, I thanked them for their kindness and friendship. As it was getting late, I became concerned they would lose their reservation. But they didn't leave. I watched as the family busied themselves with a few groceries and odds and ends while the tire was put on the rack for the spare.

"Now that you have a spare," Grandmother said, "we should all go over to the Cracker Barrel and have ourselves a nice dinner. We'd like you to come with us, if you'd like."

A good meal sounded like a dream. I could pay for the dinner, thanking them for their help and unconditional support.

Right after being seated, Grandpa Dave led the family in a prayer of thanksgiving for the bountiful meal. Everyone was thankful for the blessings of the day, especially me. During the meal, gracious conversation with plenty of corny jokes entertained us.

When I attempted to pay for the meal Grandma said, "That's out of the question."

"But you've done so much. It would be my way to do something for the family."

"Nonsense! We had a very pleasant day. After all, you did provide our afternoon entertainment."

Hearty laughter broke out. I hated to see the meal end or think about them leaving. They made me feel as if I were part of their family. It doesn't get any better than that.

Walking out to the parking lot, Hilary approached, "We always stay in a campground on Saturday night because we attend a church service on Sunday morning. Would you like to go with us? We'd be happy to come and pick you up."

I didn't ask what denomination. I didn't care. The family had clearly shown an example of Christianity in action. I accepted the gracious offer, knowing that the three generations that I had the privilege getting to know, didn't get that way by accident.

It was another bright day when the family parked alongside the camper the next morning. Poking my head into the Caravan, I saw everyone dressed in their Sunday best. The moment felt good as the family made room for me, like I belonged.

As the Caravan approached the church, I noticed a sign by the entrance, "Faith Baptist Church." The church had a contemporary flair and was set back from the road on a large lot. People began to gather on the outside platform by the church's doors. It was a simple church that held a couple hundred folks, nothing pretentious. However, the ambiance grabbed your spirit, from the time we walked in until the time we left. After a couple of hymns and a prayer, the minister began his lesson. I found his comments rather spooky. He spoke about our Christian duty toward one another; brotherly love should be extended even when it's not convenient.

Wasn't this what just happened to me or am I dreaming? God must have prepared his lesson.

My insides exploded with joy. I wanted to jump up and tell everyone about my experience. As great as I felt, I held my words, not wanting to embarrass the family. After the service, we gathered around the church's sign for a few pictures, sharing the customary chuckles as we responded with smiles to the word *cheese.* Too soon it was time to go back to the camper. We exchanged email addresses and said our goodbyes. Their goodbyes left me with a grateful but heavy heart.

With our Lord's perfect timing, everything had been placed in motion before it ever happened. The family was only minutes away at the time of the mishap. Could this have been a coincidence? I don't believe there are any coincidences with God.

Chapter 29

A little before eight on Monday morning, I drove to the ABC dealership. Unfamiliar streets, scads of traffic and the fear of getting the motor home in another tight jam twisted my face into a grimace. Businesses, a considerable distance from the road, allowed clusters of signs to own the street. I looked back and forth across the four lane highway in search of ABC's familiar sign. As I gawked, horns blew and traffic dashed around me. My snail's pace had spawned some interesting conversations and cranky looks from the drivers.

For someone who would rather have an easygoing uncomplicated life, I could sure get myself in a lot of trouble. Having to confront ABC with the tire caused most of my immediate problems. My stomach rumbled in agreement. I eased over into the right lane when I spotted the sign.

I assumed they'd have a lot large enough for a motor home. Not so! I managed to get a little more than half of the camper into the drive; the rest hung in the street like a target. Going forward only allowed a narrow opening between cars. Even if it were possible, it would take an expert to navigate through that maze. I sure didn't fall into that category.

I could see an open space in front of the bay doors. I searched for a different route, and I noticed a parking lot across from ABC that would give me a clear shot at the doors. That's once they moved everything. I held my breath as I flirted with

171

disaster. I put on my warning lights and slowly backed into the road. As I didn't hear a crash or squealing brakes, I felt I had managed the maneuver.

"Thank you, Father," I sighed.

By the time I got to the parking lot, I needed a shower. The dealership could figure out the rest.

The pungent odor of too many tires escaped from my back bin as I opened the door. With effort, I lifted the heavy, steel-belted piece out of the bin and I marched into the store. A brawny man in his late thirties, who towered over me by at least a foot and a half, asked what I wanted.

I'm standing here struggling to hang onto some heavy tread, do you think I'm selling girl scout cookies?

I grunted as I swung the ragged piece onto the counter, and I began explaining my situation.

"I don't understand why this tire blew when it only has sixteen thousand miles on it. You can check the wear on my other tires. You'll find they've been well taken care of."

He examined the tread on the separation and agreed. He said he would have to check to be sure that something else, like a nail, hadn't caused the problem.

"Everything goes through ABC, so I'll have to file a report with them.

"I'll complete it after the tire has been checked."

I can't do anything until they authorize it." He pulled out a blank form and slapped it on the counter for me to sign.

172

My gut feeling told me another snow job lay ahead. Regardless, the coach had to be checked, along with the brake lines, so I signed the form. The image of white material billowing behind the coach assured me it had been a pretty violent separation.

"Well, we'll check the coach for you, but I can tell you right now that ABC isn't going to replace this tire or do anything about it."

"What?"

"It's their policy that when tires on a motor home are three years old they should be replaced, regardless of mileage. Your chassis is a 1999 which makes it older than that."

"Yes, but the coach is a 2000," I countered.

"Sorry ma'am, we have to go with the age shown by the VIN number. I'll still fill out the report and check the coach. I just wanted you to know that ABC isn't going to do anything about it."

I pulled out the manual to find the warranty while I waited. Unfortunately, my manual had nothing listed on motor homes, only cars.

If they can't do anything until they have approval the work won't get done, unless I want to spend days in their waiting room.

Not much I can do about it but you'd think that rather than take a chance on irritating a customer, wouldn't it be good business to accommodate a feisty, mature woman?

And what about some concern like we're sure glad you weren't hurt or sorry for the inconvenience. It looks like I've been put in the wrong category again. He thinks I'm just a hard of hearing old lady who doesn't have the energy to climb into the RV, much less put up a stink.

As difficult as it was to remain polite, I had ventured a long way from home. I needed to be practical. Getting nasty wouldn't get the coach checked.

"We'll see what the company has to say about that," I said.

I'll get results no matter how long it takes.

Replacing tires every three years regardless of condition seemed ridiculous. What would be the point of warranties for forty, fifty, and sixty thousand miles? I stood in a huff by the front desk for ten minutes. No one bothered to approach me. They were probably letting me cool off after I learned about their policy.

A workman approached, "Ma'am, would you please pull the motor home over in front of the bay doors? We'll clear the way for you. Then we'll check everything and let you know what we find."

To avoid the overpowering odor from the tires that surrounded their work areas, I waited in the coach. As soon as I felt someone under the camper, I went out to critique the inspection. I walked around the outside until I saw a pair of legs sticking out.

"How does it look?"

"I'm almost finished here, ma'am, but so far everything looks great," the man hollered.

"And the tires—are they wearing all right?"

"Yeah! The tires are in good condition and the brake lines are OK too."

Having the report I went back into the shop and relayed the message to the man at the front desk. He said he would put it in his report and promised to send me a copy, but he never did.

(When I had returned to Indiana, I checked with the ABC dealer I dealt with. He told me the warranty was for four years not three. I should contact the company again on the claim which I did. It took almost two years to collect.)

Chapter 30

Pulling out of ABC's drive, I could see Interstate 90 a few blocks ahead. As I took the ramp, I remembered that my road service would expire soon. I didn't want that to happen, especially since no one could give me a reason why the tire blew. It would've been better to have had a nail in it. Now I wondered if I was driving on faulty tires. I planned to call from the next rest area, about thirty miles away, and renew the service.

The sun continued to pound its intense heat onto the pavement. Relief occasionally became available under the towering pines that shaded portions of the highway. As I took the exit at the rest area, I could see a crowd gathered around a refreshment stand. A long table had been placed under the trees about twenty feet to the side of the restrooms. The thought of a cool glass of lemonade made my mouth water. Looking around, I saw a phone on the side of the building. It looked like the hottest spot in the park. I peeled my bare legs off of the leather seat and slid out of the cab. Hot, sticky and tired, I walked toward the phone.

With a little luck, I'll get this done quickly.

After dialing the number on my card, a recording announced my choices. I pushed the appropriate number and reached a live person. As I could barely hear the woman, I pushed the *loud* button at the top of the phone. A low decibel female voice responded. I explained that I had a severe hearing loss, hoping that she would speak up or enunciate clearly. However, the quality of her voice didn't change. I gave her the numbers on my card and told her I wanted to renew my coverage. After she checked the numbers, she insisted that I didn't have a policy with her company.

Knowing she was mistaken, I said, "Your company authorize a tow truck to change a tire for me two days ago on Interstate 90. If I don't have coverage, why would they do that?"

She continued to insist that I didn't have coverage. "How can you expect to renew a policy you don't have?" she asked.

I have coverage.

Several minutes of frustration ensued, trying to convince her I did have coverage. To make matters worse, she talked while I talked. I couldn't understand what she said. I repeated the conversation to be certain that I understood her. This brought a snotty tone to her voice. Realizing I wasn't going to give up, she gave me an alternative. I could buy a new policy.

"Fine!" I said. *Why didn't she say this ten minutes ago?*

"But you'll have to fill out a new application. First of all, I'll need the address of the place where you are calling from."

"There is no address here. I'm calling from a rest area."

This scene had to be coming from a Bud Abbott and Lou Costello act.

With drinks in hand, the crowd began to gather around.

"I can't give you a policy without an address."

Carolee O'Neill

"I can give you my home address, but there is no address here. I'm in the middle of the wilderness!"

The conversation became more and more redundant, and I became more and more cantankerous.

About the time I was ready to slam the receiver into its cradle, a man tapped me on the shoulder, "Do you want me to talk to that person? I'm from these here parts."

I wanted to kiss him. "Yes! Yes! That would be fantastic."

"Hello ma'am. This here place is known as Quartz Flats. It's out in the middle of nowhere, so there's no address here."

Before long, the poor fellow had become just as frustrated as I. Behind us, several people were shaking their heads, while others were chuckling. By the time my rescuer obtained the new policy number, we both were drenched from the heat. As he handed me the information, I was so grateful that I shook his hand several times. Once again, I had been blessed with someone to help me when I needed it most. Another comedy, or was it just another day in the world of RVing?

Although I was ready to curl up and sleep for the rest of the day, I decided to make my Spokane destination. Traveling west, the terrain began to change from green valleys to a desert motif as I entered the State of Washington. The mountains were now a backdrop for the sandy soil that sprouted its desert grass.

Just outside of Spokane the traffic got as thick as ants on honey. My watch read four in the afternoon.

With all the confusion, I had forgotten I had crossed another time zone. I sat smack in the middle of rush hour traffic. Cars sped past on a road that seemed to narrow after a long day. Keeping the motor home centered between the yellow and white lines at a respectable fifty-five miles an hour had turned into a painstaking task.

Suddenly, the vehicle swayed, an old familiar sound reverberated through the coach.

My foot hit the brake and my grip tightened on the steering wheel.

"Not again!" I whimpered.

In a fraction of a second, I glanced between the two side mirrors, checking for a safety net. The narrow shoulder sloped toward a deep ditch.

Fine, black gravel made up its covering, a poor place to park a motor home. Not having a choice, I put on my hazard lights, easing the camper off the inch and a half curb that ran along the highway. The traffic continued as though nothing had happened, coming so close that I couldn't open the cab door. The slant of the shoulder made it impossible to exit on the passenger's side. It would be a straight shot right to the bottom of the ditch, taking the black dirt with me. Sooner or later there had to be a break in traffic. I'd have to be patient.

Being tipped toward the ditch, gravity caused the cab door to be very heavy. When I saw an opening, I pushed the door as hard as I could with both my hands and my feet. I squeezed through the available space. Then I went around to the front of the camper. This time I didn't hesitate to check all the tires. The inside tire on the passenger's side was as smooth as a baby's behind. Spellbound, I stared at a tire that still held its air.

How can this happen? These tires were just checked a few hours ago. Getting help in all this traffic is going to be impossible.

In spite of the problems renewing the road service, I said a prayer of thanksgiving. On top of that one, another prayer put my dilemma in the hands of my heavenly Father. While I walked to the rear of the unit, the traffic didn't wince—and they weren't looking my way. I began waving my arms in a jumping jack fashion, thinking it worked the first time. The wind from the cars whipped my bare legs with fine sand as I did my routine. My concern grew as the moments passed. After about ten minutes of worrying, waving and jumping, my little prayer had slid into the shadow of doubt. David's cousin, Alice, used to tell me that I'd give a job to God, but then I'd take it right back again. I chuckled at the memory, realizing she was right. I decided to counteract the worrying by repeating, *everything is in Divine Order—everything is in Divine Order.*

In between the waving and the jumping, I looked down the road for the separation. But I didn't spot anything. This one was gone forever.

Standing alongside of the road, I felt like crying, knowing I'd just get a dirty face and swollen eyes.

A tap on the shoulder startled me.

I let out a yelp and jumped.

The lanky fair-skinned youth, who had come to my rescue, accompanied me with his jump. For a brief moment he stared at me, like I was the Boston Strangler.

Staying where he had landed, he asked, "Do you need some help, ma'am?"

I wanted to hug him, but with the look on his face I kept my distance.

"That would be wonderful, thank you!"

I locked the camper and walked with Troy to where his mom had parked. A late model BMW was sitting in front of the camper. Troy opened the passenger's door as I bent over and introduced myself to the young woman behind the wheel. I told her of the previous separation with this being my second in two days.

"Oh brother," she said. "Come on, get in and please call me Diana."

Pushing her shoulder length light brown hair back, she put on her sunglasses, "We'll be happy to get you to a phone and help you contact road service."

Troy climbed into the back, offering me the front seat of the black coupe. Diana looked over her shoulder to check the traffic. Never hesitating, I got into the car. Fear of bodily harm hadn't entered my mind. Again, I had been blessed with good people.

With directional on, Diana drove the BMW on the shoulder, increasing her speed. The traffic flowed like water down the rapids as cars began to veer to the left. The BMW rocked as it crossed the edge of the highway, spitting stones as it matched the speed of the oncoming traffic.

181

Diana spoke of her life as a teacher and I talked about my adventure. In this relaxed atmosphere, time passed quickly. Before I knew it, we were at the off-ramp. As we exited, a convenience store was to our left with phones visible on the outside of the building. Diana cut across traffic and drove into the store's lot. I handed her the road service number obtained earlier that day.

The black of the phones mimicked the condition of the store. Outlined in the store's dirt laden windows were stacks of pop cans. The sidewalk was defaced with oil spots, discarded cigarette butts and flattened chewing gum. Diana ignored the unsightly environment, lifted the receiver, and dialed the number.

Sure hope she doesn't get the same woman I got this morning.

Diana completed the call without a problem. Within minutes, we were back on the highway, heading toward the motor home via a five mile detour.

The westbound traffic had eased a bit when we circled back, but the sun still burned brightly. As we walked to the rear of the coach, I noticed an emergency vehicle coming down the highway, lights flashing. Pulling up behind the camper, a blonde, stout young man with a deep tan grinned as he walked toward us.

"You folks OK?"

I told him that Diana and Troy had saved my day and that a tow truck should be on its way.

He tipped his visor and said, "Just wanted to make sure you had help. If you're sure you're OK, I'll be on my way."

"I'm fine, but thanks for stopping."

Capturing a space in traffic, he darted around us with his emergency lights flashing.

As I watched him speed away, I asked Diana if I could give her something for gas or her time.

"No, you don't owe me anything," she replied. "What you can do is to help someone else, pass it on."

"That's not a problem. I've spent my life doing that."

"Well then, maybe it's pay-back time."

As the tow truck pulled to the side of the road behind the RV, I said, "Everything is in Divine Order, isn't it?"

Diana chuckled, "Look at the name on the tow truck."

I turned. In bold letters was printed "Divine's Service."

Amazed I stood speechless.

A fellow in a gray, one-piece work suit approached us. I showed him the separation, asking if he would be safe changing it with the motor home on such an angle.

"I'll be fine, ma'am," he replied, going right to work.

Between the heat and the wind from the passing cars, the grayish-black soot soon covered the man, except for the circles of white around his eyes. Trails of perspiration made a pathway down his neck, ending in black beads. Regardless, he

183

continued his labor. I must admit that deep inside I hoped that Divine's Service would consider the deplorable conditions this man had to work under when they prepared their bill.

Feeling drained, I asked Diana and Troy if they'd like to see the coach. Although Troy hadn't complained, his damp forehead and flushed face said he'd be delighted to get out of the sun. Entering the coach, I slipped off my sooty tennis shoes and brushed off my white socks, now gray. Both my guests followed my example. I gave them the grand tour, from the queen-size bed to the generator.

Diana later told me that Troy had concerns about stopping. "I told him, of course, I'm going to stop."

"I'm sure glad you did! I guess I must've looked a little crazy, jumping up and down out there."

Diana laughed, "Perhaps…harmless?"

I could understand Troy's concern, especially today. However, his mom's courage set an example he'd never forget.

After Divine's Service left, we exchanged email addresses. I followed them to the nearest WalMart. I had made my destination for the night, the hard way. Everything was in Divine Order.

Chapter 31

Upon hearing the stories about the tire separations, the WalMart manager checked the tire. "Sorry ma'am, but Missoula gave you the wrong tire. We don't carry a tire big enough for your motor home. If you tell me what kind of tires you want, I'll call around to see who carries them."

Noticing that I had ABC's brand on the camper, he asked if I would like to go to them.

"No way! They told me that their company wasn't about to do anything about the first tire. I need reliable tires, and I don't feel theirs meet the bill. In the past, I've had excellent service from Discount Tire with my cars and my husband's truck. Do they have a store around here?"

"There's a Discount Tire about three miles away. I'll call and make sure they have the right tires for you."

As I'd already been taken a few times, I called my nephew in St. Louis. Michael had been in charge of training and the repairs on army vehicles. He knew his mechanics. Tires were a no-brainer.

"Look at the side of the tires that are on it," Michael said. "And don't settle for anything less. I'm sure that with the size of your unit you'll need something in the neighborhood of a ten ply."

I gave the information to the service manager at WalMart. Discount Tire would have seven new tires to put on my unit in the morning. Until then, WalMart would be my host for the rest of the evening.

Carolee O'Neill

At eight o'clock the next morning, I drove into Discount Tire's lot. Within an hour I had six new tires on the coach and a seventh on the rack for a spare. I felt safe. I'd soon be in Bremerton, Washington, with the ocean a breath away.

After Ellensburg, Washington, the terrain changed from a desert motif to mountains of evergreens clad with soft shadows from the partially cloudy sky. It felt good to be on my way again. Bridges crossed the remains of mountain creeks as the water trickled over their rocky beds. Unclaimed beauty climbed high over granite crevices covered with snow. Majestic splendor surrounded me. The Creator had used His perfect paint brush to complete His splendor. There weren't enough waysides or enough time to absorb the design that engulfed my soul in these mountains.

Esther and Charlie's home butted up against the shores of the Puget Sound. Doves cooed and gulls sang in the early morning as Esther and I ate breakfast on the deck. The weather obliged, allowing us to enjoy most of our meals in a shaded area close to the water.

Esther's daughter Liz and her husband Tony provided a parking space for the camper along their retaining wall. a perfect spot indeed. I could even extend the slide. Tony offered to help me level the coach. I didn't need to use the jacks.

Esther had planned two weeks of entertainment and good food. A sightseeing trip took us to Victoria, British Columbia, by way of a ferry, introducing me to beautiful landscaping, the delicacies of Canada, the incredible Butchart Gardens and a tour of the magnificent Empress Hotel.

We considered the afternoon tea until we realized that it would be fifty dollars per person. Even at Canadian dollars that seemed a little steep for a few finger sandwiches, a couple of scones on a fancy plate, and, of course, tea. Others must have agreed as the dining room held few guests. We smiled and I almost curtsied as we left.

The fields on Washington's northern shore were in bloom with lavender. Their scent saturated the air for miles. At the festival, everything had been made with it—soap, ice cream, perfume even the cheesecake. Of course, we had to try the cheesecake. Then we drove to one of Esther's favorite places for lunch, called "3 Crabs." She hadn't been there since Charlie died, so it would be a treat for both of us.

Delighted to be with her, even though Charlie had recently died, we shared moments that made the look in her eyes twinkle into a smile. She told stories about all the babies that Charlie delivered, all the happy couples, and all the joy that he had brought into her life. Listening to her fantasize about her prince on a white horse, refreshed the goodness in my own memories. I didn't have to bask in the trauma that surrounded David and Hospice or the disease that had drained our lives. For now I could rest in her vision.

One morning, as we ate breakfast on the deck, Esther pointed toward distant waters. Tony approached in his kayak. Ripples drifted across the still water as his paddle dipped on one side and then the other.

What a peaceful way to start the day. Look how easily he glides. I'd never be able to do that. He's so smooth with those paddles.

Within moments Tony was on shore, walking our way. "Good morning," he hollered across the yard.

"Good morning! That's an interesting sport. You make it look so easy, but I'm sure it's not."

"It is, really. Would you like to try it?"

"No…No! I'd never be able to get in or out of the kayak."

"That's not a problem. Liz and I will help you. How about four o'clock this afternoon?"

I looked at Esther, hoping she would rescue me, but no. She thought I should do it. I didn't protest too much. How could I refuse such an intriguing experience? Besides, I'd never have another opportunity and I wanted to seize every moment. At four fifteen, Liz and Tony were lowering me into the kayak. To my dismay, Tony waded in the slippery weeds that lay wasted from the outgoing tide. One shove and I was ocean bound.

Liz came alongside of me in her kayak, teaching me how to use the paddles. "Keep your elbows close to your body and dip one oar at a time."

I had to be doing something right because I glided forward with ease. Unbelievable peace filled my soul. The smooth sea rippled as the tip of the paddle touched the sea. Esther and Tony stood on shore, like parents watching a child on a new adventure.

Then I looked into the transparent waters. Thick, slimy weeds waved with the current. The hair on my neck bristled. The sight reminded me of my older sister. As a small child, I loved to float on my inner tube at my grandma's lake cottage.

One day without warning, my sister came running down the limestone steps to the lake, screaming, "The weeds are going to grab you and pull you down to the bottom. You have to get out of there."

Terror whirled through my young body.

In a panic, arms and legs splashed along side of the inner tube, in an attempt to reach shore.

The motion spun me in circles. Somehow I got to shore, forever to be haunted by the weeds my sister had planted in my head.

"We'll stay close to shore so you can wade back if you have to," Liz said.

"I'd rather not have to look at these weeds. They're giving me the creeps."

"OK, if you're sure."

I shared my wretched sister experience with her in great detail.

Liz laughed, "Having five brothers and sisters, I understand what you mean."

As we went toward deeper waters, not a sound shattered the silence. Unforgettable sights held my attention, like tall stately evergreens, a log home, and other homes that hovered over the sea, boasting adequate room for many guests. As we glided across the glass like surface, I thanked God

189

Carolee O'Neill

for these peaceful moments. With Him at my side, I had stepped forward into the unknown. Once again, He made it worthwhile.

Before I left, Esther compiled an agenda for my trip. I should stop at Mount Rainier, Mount St. Helens, drive the Oregon coast and see the Columbian River Gorge. She assured me the gorge would be the highlight of my trip. In August of 2003, I left Esther's home. As usual, time went too fast. I had driven many miles to see her, a feat in itself. However, the hours spent on the road evaporated into spaces that filled my mind with remembrances for the years to come.

Upon arriving at Longview, Washington, I took some pictures for my brother after I crossed the bridge into Oregon. He loved living in Longview.

Before the road jotted out toward the ocean, I spotted a bakery. I never pass a bakery without a gander. When I opened their door, I knew heaven had arrived. Real cream puffs filled the case. If I could've found a way to preserve them, I would've bought a dozen—maybe two. My mouth watered as I prepared myself for a taste from the past.

Every time I visited my grandparents in Cicero, we went to my favorite bakery. The whipped cream cakes, donuts and pastries were made from scratch right before our eyes. Grandpa would lift me up to the countertop so I could watch the donuts being glazed. As soon as they were placed on the plate the crullers made a puddle of sweet frosting. Then Grandpa would tell me to close my eyes. He'd place something in my hand that ran warm rivers of sweetness into my palm. Of course, we had to have a pastry while we waited for the baker to finish our whipped cream cake. A freshly glazed donut did the trick just fine. Who could ever forget those whipped cream cakes? I took my prize to the motor home. Licking my fingers, I savored its final goodness. I sat overlooking the ocean, aware that it's the simple things in life which bring us the greatest joy.

As I traveled down the Oregon coast, glimpses of the ocean could be seen. The Pacific looked gray—foreboding, not its usual deep blue. Fog had captured most views. I decided to turn north toward the Columbian River Gorge. Bridal Veil and Multnomah Falls were on the Oregon side of the impressive river. Numerous signs announced the three bridges that crossed to the Washington side. I decided to cross the gorge on "The Bridge of the Gods." I wondered if it had been named after a mythological character. It would be interesting to learn the actual meaning of that title.

When I paid my toll, I saw a sign that read, "Speed Limit Fifteen Miles an Hour." I laughed, but not for long.

As I began to cross, the steel plates of the bridge treated me to a slippery-type of a sensation.

I wasn't laughing when I couldn't get up to fifteen miles an hour, either.

It must be the distance to the water that's making me feel like I'm sliding.

191

Carolee O'Neill

The steel girders looked strong, but would they hold a sliding motor home?

Tingles made every hair on my body stand at attention. A low whimper crept from my throat as I tried to look and yet not to. Torn between enjoying the moment, seeing the view and staying alive, I took quick peeks up and down the river.

Perspiration lined my grip on the steering wheel as my hands attempted a strong hold that quickly weakened with each turn of the camper's tires. As I waited for something to come from the other way, my heart banged like a basketball being run down a gym floor, but nothing did.

At the end of this memorable drive a sign read, "One-Way Bridge." Sure wish I would've known that before I crossed.

"The Bridge of the Gods" had earned its name, much higher and I could have shaken hands with Him.

Not long after the gorge, highway 97 turned northward, away from the river. The scenery changed. Barren hills climbed to four thousand feet.

By mid-afternoon, I came upon a straightaway where several cars were parked. People were looking toward the horizon with binoculars. Being a curious soul, I stopped.

One elderly gentleman pointed, "Look, you can see all four mountains. They look like they are in a row, Mount Hood, Mount Rainier, Mount Adams, and Mount St. Helens. That's the one that looks like somebody took a bite out of it." We laughed as we shared the wonder, another unbelievable day.

Since I'd had the second tire separation, the thought that others could have the same problems bothered me. As my route took me back through Missoula, Montana, I decided to stop and tell ABC about the second separation, even though I didn't have the separation.

Right after I walked through their front door, I was confronted by a man who was too young to be so nasty. He didn't care that I had had the second separation. Smugly, he said, "ABC isn't going to do anything about it, so you can complain all you want."

"I didn't stop to complain. I stopped so others wouldn't get hurt using your faulty tires. If you want a war, buddy, you picked a good day to have one because I'm up to it. Your smart mouth just earned first place in the letter I intend to write to the company."

The scene got everyone's attention. I held my ground, staring into his face without a blink. No one moved. The secretary turned gray.

With clenched fists and a frown that went all the way down to my chin, I snarled, "It may take awhile, but I assure you, I will win and you will lose!"

I turned and cast a glare at the people standing around the room, marched to the door and slammed it on my way out. I continued my attention grabbing march to the motor home. I mentally patted myself on the back for standing up for what I thought was right.

Chapter 32

Knowing I'd never come this way again, or at least not for a long time, I set my sights on Mount Rushmore, the Black Hills and the Badlands. I surveyed the map for altitude in an attempt to avoid getting sick as much as possible. By the time I reached Billings, Montana, where Interstate 94 and 90 split, I had been over the Continental Divide again. My body should have manufactured some extra red blood cells with this trip. That piece of nursing knowledge had my brain convinced that I shouldn't have a problem. I headed for the mountains.

My previous research showed that if I wanted to see Mount Rushmore and the Black Hills, highway 14/16 off of 90 would take me there. I breezed along, enjoying the scenery, until the road split. Dilemma time.

Which way should I go?

At fifty-five miles an hour, I only had a second to make a decision. A sign read, "16 Mount Rushmore." It had to be the right way. So I turned onto 16. Within a few miles, the narrow road had a distant vanishing point on the horizon. I became concerned. Few cars passed and signs weren't present along the desert motif, with no place to turn around. Had the decision to take 16 been wrong or right? I would soon know.

Ten miles later, the road began to climb. I was gaining altitude too fast for comfort.

Huge evergreens peeked out of the thick brush at different angles, sometimes covering the road.

The highway turned quickly, cliffs sheared to a depth I didn't want to consider.

Any extra red blood cells that I had manufactured were traveling a road all their own.

I stomped on the accelerator.

The motor grabbed its power and soared upward. Adrenaline shot outward through my veins to mimic its speed.

I had demanded too much power to control the camper. My foot hit the brake to slow the coach as I crested the hill.

In a breath, I was heading downward. I shifted into low gear.

Back and forth, the camper swayed as it obeyed my commands around the sharp curves and shallow dips.

Over and over again, I stared at hair-pin curves with nothing more than a ten-foot guard rail between me and eternity.

My backend slammed on the road in disapproval of the quick dips.

Don't ride your brakes. You'll burn them out.

The motor groaned in low gear as it held back its fifteen thousand pound burden against the steep downhill grind.

A car approached. My muscles ached as I slowed the coach.

I can't give an inch. He's smaller than I am. He'll have to figure it out.

Carolee O'Neill

Beads of perspiration ran down my back as I glanced at the car and saw it off on the inside shoulder.

Again, the road began to climb, straight up. I whimpered as I envisioned another decent.

God must have known my route because by the time I got to the top, I saw a sign, "Beaver Lake Campground."

For some strange reason, I didn't care how much it cost. I drove in, parked, and allowed myself ten minutes to shake before I registered.

A stooped elderly gentleman with stiff gray hair that didn't lay down, stood behind the registration desk. "Howdy, my name is Mike and I need to register you and your husband, ma'am."

Feeling a little crazy, "That's going to be hard, because he's dead."

Startled, Mike looked up from the register and glared at me in surprise. A long pause followed my smart aleck remark. People at the snack bar glanced my way.

"You drove up here by yourself?"

"Sure did, and I must admit it was the drive of a lifetime. Don't want to repeat that performance. Once was enough."

"Ma'am, highway 16 is just about the worst way you could have gotten here, especially with the size motor home you're drivin'."

As the conversation continued, more people began to gather, mumbling to each other. I guessed they wanted to take a good look at a crazy woman.

"Mike, I didn't know that before I took 16. I saw a sign that said Mt. Rushmore. That's where I

196

wanted to go, so I took it. Won't do that again, but somehow with the grace of the good Lord, I made it. He must have some important plans for me."

When I realized I had become a conversation piece, I said, "You do what you have to do. Besides, the only way out was up, so I went for it."

The group laughed. A lady holding her companion's hand said, "I sure give you credit for forging ahead with a motor home. I don't think I could ever do it."

"I thank you, ma'am, but you probably could've. All you have to do is set your mind to it and be a little crazy. I set out for adventure and to live life to its fullest. Of course, this drive had a little more adventure than I bargained for. I encourage you all to do the same thing—do what's in your heart. If you're standing before St. Peter, you'll know it's too late to do that.

Let me tell you that after caring for a dying spouse, a person realizes that life is very short. I wanted to explore as much of this land as I could before I landed in the happy hunting grounds. Which, by the way, I thought would happen on my way up here. But then a trip like that is what memories are made of. Right?" The group nodded and laughed, "It also makes great material for storytelling."

"These are the kind of stories that our grandparents used to tell us when we were kids. I never believed them, but I sure do now. I bet you all can remember a story or two about the depression."

They looked to others in affirmation.

197

Mike held up a map saying, "So you can continue to tell your stories, I'll show you a safe way to get to Mount Rushmore through the Black Hills. If you had a car, you could take a day or two and drive these squiggle lines, but not in a motor home. Anytime you see something like these on a big map, you can bet your boots that it's not the best road. When you leave here, you follow this road and don't go any other way because it will be worse than what you just came through."

My listening skills were at attention. I didn't want to repeat the same up, down, and around trip without a glance at the scenery.

"Well…you made it here okay and that's what counts. I'm sure you're tired. I'll help you get into your space and get set up."

A case of altitude sickness spent the night or a panic attack? Whatever it was, I got a nice *clean* start in the morning.

After all the excitement on highway 16, Mount Rushmore, the Black Hills and the Badlands were an anti-climax.

Mike mentioned that I missed the best part of the Black Hills because I didn't have a car. I have to look into this. Having reached the outer limits of fear, my adrenals are "performing the way God designed them." There isn't much that can surprise me anymore. The rest has to be a downhill ride. Wait a minute! I better keep that thought at bay. The last time I made a remark like that God corrected me. Not long afterwards, David got his diagnosis. I found out the hard way that I had a lot to learn.

Chapter 33

Of course, I imagined the worst possible scenario about towing a car. Gas stations kept the juices flowing.

How will I be able to get in and out with all that length? Either the car will be sitting in the driving area or I'll be too far from the pump. All I need to do is whack the side of the car with one of them. That wouldn't make my insurance man happy. He's probably wishing he never would've written the policy in the first place. I sure can't count on a Flying J's truck stop being available every time I need gas, either. I'm getting way ahead of myself. First I have to find a car and do some more research on tow bars.

Every campground had lots of campers who towed cars. Again, they were more than happy to give their opinions on the easiest to handle. Hands down, the Falcon tow bar by RoadMaster fit the bill.

Now I needed a car. The Saturn and the Honda both had engines that were programmed for towing without adding special parts. I decided on the Honda CRV because it fit just right as I backed into the seat. I found one in Michigan that was a year old, thus avoiding the new car smell that give my sinuses fits. As I had researched the cost of the vehicle, I knew the sticker price was fair. However, I wanted to know more.

"Why is this car so expensive?" I asked. "It's much more than the Saturn and it would work just as well. Besides, I'd be getting better gas mileage."

"Maybe," John said. "But this one has four-wheel drive, and it's easier to get in and out of."

"I don't need four-wheel drive. I'll never use it. Don't they make them without it?"

"No! I'm sorry, but if you want this CRV, then you're stuck with the four-wheel drive."

"Granted, four-wheel drive has its place when you get into trouble like David did in the Superstition Mountains. There's no way I will ever get into that much trouble."

"What happened?" John asked as he leaned his slender, six foot frame against a corner post and folded his arms across his chest.

"Keep in mind that we had just painted the truck before we left Indiana for Apache Junction, Arizona. A few days after we arrived, David ran into an old prospector who told him there was gold in 'them their hills' around Apache Lake.

Of course, we both were enthralled with the mountains and neither of us had been to Apache Lake. We thought that an afternoon drive and a little prospecting would be fun because it was only thirty miles away. On our way, we stopped at Canyon Lake to take some pictures. Right after that, a little sign warned that the road would narrow. When it did, it really didn't narrow that much. However, in another half mile the word 'narrow' took on a different meaning. Well, that didn't stop David.

There wasn't enough room for two small cars, much less a truck and a car. On top of that, the road had been graded into a washboard, leaving the edges on either side with five inch mounds of sand for guardrails. Can you imagine that? I'm only guessing, but I'd say we were on about a ten percent grade, maybe more. It was straight down.

All of a sudden, this little car came charging at us. David, being too much of a nice guy, pulled over as far as he could to let the guy pass. Well, the car passed all right, but the sand gave way on our side and the truck slid sideways into the drainage ditch. I could touch the mountain, for Pete's sake!

David's solution to the dilemma was to step on the gas. The wheels spun, and we slid further into the trench. Now the two thousand dollar paint job was within inches of getting a new look. David grumbled something under his breath.

I didn't move.

Then he jumped out of the truck. I had no idea why because he wasn't a talker. I could see that he went down in the ditch. When he got back in the truck, he stepped on the gas and we popped right out of there. I learned later that he had engaged the four-wheel drive."

"That worked out OK, didn't it?" John said.

"Yes, but the story doesn't end there. We were still in big trouble. The only way to get out of there was down. I dug my nails into the upholstery as I realized we would have to go back up on the outside of the cliff. It wasn't a pleasant day, probably the worst one of my life.

As David began his ascent, the truck shimmied on the washboard road and head toward the edge of the sandy guardrail. I screamed.

The steep upward grade prevented a view over the hood of the truck. I imagined David driving straight into a six thousand foot canyon when the road curved and we didn't.

I screamed louder—'Let me out! Let me out!'

He ignored me as he pulled himself high with the steering wheel to see over the hood.

I screamed again, each time with a higher pitch as fear controlled my vocal chords.

I shouted—'Stop! Let me out.'

He yelled; I can't! You'll fall off the cliff.

Believe me that didn't help. You'd think with all that screaming, he would've stopped just to get rid of me. But no, he kept right on going and I kept right on screaming. By the time he had gotten to where he could stop, both of our nervous systems had had a good workout. Now you can understand what I mean when I say I'll never get myself in that much trouble."

"By the way," John asked, "Did you find any gold?"

"You're kidding, right? We didn't even get to Apache Lake."

John chuckled, "But the four-wheel drive did save your neck, right?"

"Yeah, I suppose."

"Unfortunately, this CRV still has four wheel drive. It's automatic and it'll only engage if you ever manage to get yourself in trouble. After that story, you'll probably never use it."

"Guess you're right. It's a nice-looking vehicle, so let's go with it."

Now came the hardest part. My 1985 Mercedes Roadster would have to be sold to purchase the Honda. I kept telling myself it was only a car, but such a nice car. Heads turned as I drove down the street. The chrome bumper against the polished cranberry finish flashed in the sunlight. With the top down, the light-gray leather upholstery and the custom dash announced the rest of its elegance. It had saved the day on many occasions.

When David's son had been critically injured, the Mercedes took us from Apache Junction, Arizona, to Fort Worth, Texas, in record time. Of course, I drove. David didn't know how fast until a repairman in Tucson said, "Doesn't this car glide just as smooth as silk at one hundred miles an hour?"

Not realizing that David was standing behind me, I did a Jackie Gleason special, "Yeah, how sweet it is." Laughing, I turned to find myself face-to-face with a husband who was not smiling.

I cried inside as I babied my Mercedes for the last time with a good wax job. It hadn't taken long to sell. Why would it? The neighbors whispered that the new owners were getting a cream puff. They didn't think I knew that?

As David and I had purchased the Reese hitch for the Mountain Aire from Dan's, a company in Elkhart, Indiana, I decided to deal with them for my tow bar. With knees knocking, I stood at the counter. A young man approached and ask if he could help me. I wanted to say no and run for my life, but my brain insisted that I stay.

I began my attack, "I want to warn you."
He smiled.

"I have never towed a car and the thought of it is making me sick. I guess I need some help making sure that I have the right tow bar. So this is how it's going to work. I buy a set-up. You teach me how to use it until I can do it on my own, no matter how long it takes. Then you'll have to go with me for a test drive until I'm comfortable driving on my own."

"Sold," Bill said with a grin on his face.

Surprised at his instant response, I asked, "Are you sure?"

"Sure am! If you've been driving that big motor home, towing a car will be a piece of cake. You'll be surprised when you see how easy it is. And we'll stick with you until you are comfortable."

Now that I was experienced with tall tales, I didn't believe a word of it. But I needed to buy it someplace, and they had been fair to us with the fifth wheel. The day after I met with Bill, I dropped the car off to have the set-up installed. The next day I went back with the camper. I watched as they lined the car up with the motor home. All it took was a couple of locks and a two inch drop to make sure the measurements for the motor home jibed with the hitch.

"It's time for your first lesson," Bill said. "There is one thing that you should never forget."

Sure! Here it comes.

"Be careful when you pull the pins out. You don't want the tow bar to drop on your foot. The weight could easily smash it."

On that note, I practiced the procedure over and over until Bill started laughing and I had a backache.

"As soon as you get tired of doing that," he chuckled, "I'll give you your road test."

To think I did without a car all last winter and this is so easy. There has to be a catch someplace. I bet the car is a nightmare to tow. It can't be this simple.

"I guess I'm ready, but I want to reserve the right to ask as many questions as I need to. Bill nodded, "You are about to be so surprised."

After I finished hooking up the car, I programmed it for towing. Bill decided to wait inside the camper.

When I jumped into the driver's seat I said, "Now what do I have to do, anything special, like with the brakes or headlights?"

"Not a thing. You folks had a fifth wheel before, but with a motor home it's different. Everything is ready to go."

The parking lot had plenty of room. At least I wouldn't hit anything the first trip around.

"Now look in your side mirror as we go around in a circle. Can you see the tires moving on the car?"

"Yes!"

"That means that it's been programmed correctly. Otherwise, they wouldn't be moving and the car would skid. See, it follows just like a duckling after a mama duck—simple as pie."

"Yeah, but we are still in the parking lot, so that's easy to say."

Carolee O'Neill

"Hit the road. If your camper clears the corner the car will."

With ease, the car followed just like Bill said. Excited with my new purchase, my mind planned my next trip. First it would be Lexington, Kentucky, to see the thoroughbreds, then on to the Great Smoky Mountains. Now I could go anywhere, even a trip down coastal highway one in California.

Chapter 34

I stopped at the Chamber of Commerce just before I got to Lexington, Kentucky. Not having a navigator, I wanted to study some routes before I ventured out. I hadn't planned on staying too long because autumn had begun to color the forest in the Great Smoky Mountains. I couldn't think of a better place to spend my favorite time of the year.

The gal at the Chamber yellowed the roads on the map I was supposed to follow to see the different stables.

"You can't miss them because of the tall steeples and white fences. However, some do have black fences. It all depends on the owner's likes and dislikes. It's quite simple. You won't get lost." She assured me.

Looking at the map, I saw a whole lot of distance between those yellow lines. Being close to the city, those had to be other roads. Pulling the coach onto the street, multiple side roads and major highways soon filled in the empty spaces. Then the road forked and I didn't know which way to go, but I went anyway.

A large white steeple drew my attention to my right. I drifted toward that lane.

Horns honked.

That crunched my dream-world; however, it was hard not to look. Miles of white fence hugged the lavish, green lawns along the roadway accented by stables of white with red trim.

I've got a car on the back of this thing. I could stop someplace and take it off before I get hit.

These stables are unbelievable. The horses live better than I do. I should really take the car off the back. No, I better wait. It's my first time alone. I think I'll do that in a campground. I might need help.

I have no idea why I decided to tow a car, if I intended to be a chicken when it came to taking it off the camper. Maybe I'd be less of a scary-cat with somebody else around.

Although my plans didn't include staying in Lexington, I had ended up with a couple minor detours. The map the lady gave me took me west on highway 60 to 57 north. Then I'd take the next major road back to Lexington—sounded easy enough. Well, I drove and drove.

Any minute I'll be back in Indiana before I find route 57.

Then I saw a small sign on the bottom of a green highway sign, "To 57."

That must be my road.

The ramp ended in less than a quarter of a block in a "T" that was surrounded by wilderness. Looking at the narrow crossroad that had been repaved too many times, I glanced to my right. An arrow on a small sign pointed, "To 57." Shaking my head and laughing, I had either misunderstood or the gal at the Chamber told me the wrong road.

Oh well, it doesn't matter. If I get lost, I can always sleep in the camper.

I made my turn. Within a quarter of a mile, the road became a mini-roller coaster. The RV's backend smacked the blacktop. The ups and downs of the road came too fast. I cringed.

208

Not again.

That slowed my speed to ten miles per hour. The winding road was shrouded with trees that any lumber mill would've loved to own. Autumn had blossomed into spectacular shades of burnt orange, crimson, and gold that outlined the evergreens.

Around another sharp curve, I found myself face to face with a fifty year old truck driven by a man who should have been buried long ago.

We each hit our brakes.

His bony hands, with extended arms and stiff torso, grasped the steering wheel. There he sat, wide-eyed and rigid as a board, like he had never seen a human before.

How will he get around me with this sloping shoulder? I can see the headlines now. "Motor home driven by old lady found in ditch in Kentucky Hills."

I pulled over, but not far enough to fulfill that prophesy. As he passed, his weathered face seemed more interested in me than in the slope of the ditch.

Looking at him, his expression exposed his thoughts.

"How the devil did an old woman drivin' a camper get out here?"

After a short distance, which seemed like miles, I came upon a small town. One house and a mechanic's shop made up the population. There wasn't even a bar or a church. I pulled to the side of the road across from the shop and called to a couple of young fellows standing outside. Smiling from ear to ear, they jaunted over to the motor home together.

"Howdy, ma'am. Nice rig," they said in a thick Kentucky drawl as they looked at each other, grinned and then back at me.

"Hi, fellows. I think I'm lost, but you probably figured that."

"Yes, ma'am," they said together.

"I need to find 57. Can you help me or at least get me back to Lexington?"

Puzzled, they looked at each other. When the shorter fellow began to talk, I couldn't understand a word he said. I told them about my hearing loss. Then they began to shout. When that didn't work, they talked amongst themselves and headed back to the shop like the Spearmint gum twins.

When they returned they handed me a piece of paper with a message, "There ain't no such road round here and we should know 'cuz we've been livin' here all our lives."

On the bottom of the page, they had drawn a map, showing how to get back to Lexington. I thanked them, waving as I drove off.

As though getting lost once wasn't enough, I had to try for a second time. Hmm! Seems David used to do things like this. However, he did some whoppers like when the road dead-ended at the ocean, and the trucks skimming passed on those narrow bridges in Alabama.

This time I drove north for a short distance. The map showed it as a major road, and then I'd go west again. I wanted to see the farms, no matter what! I drove and drove, but not as far as the first time. After a considerable distance, I figured I had had enough. I turned north on a country road, but one that seemed wide enough. Unfortunately, not for long.

Why are they making this so difficult? Stop complaining. You could've taken the car off the back, but no. At least this road is wider than the last one.

To make up for the additional width, I came upon a railroad track at an unbelievable thirty degree angle. I'm talking skyward. I envisioned the tow bar at ninety degrees to accomplish the feat of getting up and over the track. I had no place to go, except up. Seems I've said that before.

As I ascended toward the top of the tracks, gravity pulled my body back in the seat. Fear stripped the few nerves I had left.

What if a train comes? That can't be possible. I bet a train hasn't run on this track for years. Yeah sure! Those crossing guards don't look old to me. Just do it. You only have one choice and that up.

I shifted into low gear to pull the weight up the grade. Approaching the top, the tracks looked loose, as though the least bit of weight would finish the job. I checked my side mirror for the car. It was still there, angle and all. The heavy metal track moved up and down, banging against the wood ties as I began to cross. With the cab across, I sighed. For some strange reason, I felt safer even though there was some twenty-seven feet of motor home behind me with a car attached. My next glance went to my downhill descent.

How am I going to get through that dip at the bottom? Dear God, I hope You're listening, because this coach doesn't bend in the middle. I know, I'm back at it again. Are You having fun yet? At least I'm good for a laugh, aren't I? If it pleases You, I need some help here. Otherwise, I could be sitting down there for a long time.

A nosedive and then the descent began. Scraping sounds spoke of the camper's displeasure as I pulled it through the dip. Visions of blacktop piled in a clump sprang into my head. A small town sheriff would not be too happy about that. Once out of trouble, I stopped to see what was left of the coach and the car. Through the grace of the good Lord, I couldn't see any noticeable damage. Not wanting to find any, I jumped into the cab, praying that would be my last challenge for the day.

Private ranches lined either side of the narrow road as I traveled northward. Over the next knoll, a chauffeur driven black limousine approached. He stopped short and tried to go around me. I put my hand out to stop him. I needed more directions and he was the only one around. He tried to be congenial, in a stuffy sort of way as he sniffed the air with his elevated nose. I guessed by the look on his face that he found my ability to top the tracks along with the size of the unit contributed to his bewilderment.

With directions in hand, I drove back toward Lexington. I never saw what I came to see, but two

trips through the woods proved to be enough for
this little camper. At least I was presented with a
couple of elegant stables, met some nice young men
and saw some magnificent autumn foliage.
Unfortunately, I scared the stuffings out of a poor
old farmer. Having enough, I headed for the Great
Smoky Mountains.

Highway 75 wound south toward Knoxville,
Tennessee, giving me glimpses of the forest.
Because of the lateness of the hour when I left
Lexington, I stayed at the WalMart in Richmond,
Kentucky, for the night. Arising early the next
morning, I went to program the car for towing and
found that the key would not turn in the ignition. I
wiggled it. I checked to see if the steering wheel
was locked. When nothing worked, I tried a familiar
approach—I panicked.

Now what did I do wrong?

Looking over the programming instructions,
I couldn't find an error. Obviously, I needed help. I
rushed as fast as an old lady can to the service
counter in WalMart.

"Sorry ma'am, there's no Honda dealers in
this area. I don't know what to tell you."

Now I'm praying! I didn't know where to go
or what to do. My head swiveled back and forth,
like a lost puppy trying to find its family. Some
time passed, I don't know how much, maybe a
minute or two. Another lady came on duty. Seeing a
distressed old woman standing on one spot, she
asked if she could help me. "I wish you could, but I
think I'm stuck. I need a Honda dealer and there
isn't one around here."

"Yeah there is," she said. "There's one right down the road that is opening its doors for the first time today. My boyfriend works there. That's how I know."

An unbelievable situation turned into a miracle. Father, this is getting spooky, but I thank You for another blessing.

She called and within a few minutes the fellows were over to check on my problem. Wouldn't you know, Honda had just issued a recall on the part for the ignition. They could have the car done in one day. I was one happy camper.

Towing the car to the Honda dealership, I knew I'd have to unhook it, probably with an audience. Being my first time alone, my hands shook some, but I was determined. I lined the two vehicles up in a straight line. The pavement slanted to the left which threw the angle on the tow bar off balance. I set the emergency on both vehicles. The fellows watched, pointing and laughing, as I went back and forth between the car and the camper.

"Sure you don't want some help?"

"No, I have to do this myself."

I hoped they couldn't see how much effort it took to unplug the electrical, and that was just the beginning. Then I unfastened both safety cables and unlocked the paddle lock that held the right pin in place. *Boy, I sure hope that left pin comes out. Get your feet out of the way so they don't get smashed— remember?*

The right pin slid out, but the left one wouldn't budge. I went to my back bin to get my rubber mallet.

I called to the fellows, "A couple good whacks with this will get it out of there."

It took more than a couple, but I wasn't about to be embarrassed. That pin would come out no matter how many whacks it would take. After what seemed like forever, it gave way to the hammering. I proudly held up the pins. The fellows cheered.

The next day, I went to pick up the car. The tow bar easily unlocked and came down to a "V" to accommodate the connection. I sprayed the pins with silicone (it had proven itself to me), hoping to make their removal easier. All hooked up, I waved a "thank you" to the fellows and drove out of the lot.

At the first stop light I questioned whether or not I had closed the back bin. I adjusted my side view mirror but couldn't bring the bin into view. Being stuck at the same light several times before, I knew I had plenty of time to do a quick check.

I shifted into park and ran to the side door. By the time I reached it, I realized that my demented brain had just gotten me in big trouble; the coach was rolling backward.

I didn't think or pray. I leaped with lightning speed into the driver's seat and slammed on the brakes.

Immediately, the light changed. In no condition to drive, I pulled to the side of the highway and turned off the motor.

I was sure the people behind me were happy to see the camper moving forward instead of backward.

Carolee O'Neill

I turned to see whom I almost met the hard way. An involuntary response whispered, "Oh no" as I watched a line of antique cars drive by. I'll never know how I missed them.

By now my guardian angel must be looking for a different job. Does anybody else do this dumb stuff? Or don't you want to talk about it?

Chapter 35

Three months in the same campground in Florida didn't work for me. Being a widow in a park where couples ruled, the ladies made certain their husbands weren't going to get too close. After a season of grief with the black water valve, a hole in the caulking for the shower that left mildew under it, and having the fellow next door guide me into a tree on my way out of my spot, my patience had had a good workout. Looking ahead, I had wanted to spend at least a week in Lexington, Kentucky. I had only seen one horse farm, the woods and the railroad tracks the last time. Besides, the northern part of the country sounded pretty good to me by the end of March.

Stopping at a rest area in Kentucky, I checked around the exterior of the unit to make sure that everything was OK. Since having that encounter with John's bumper, I have never neglected this task. As I proceeded, I noticed a puddle under the bin by the black water. Lifting the door, the odor told me it wasn't the gray water that had a leak. I checked all the valves, pushing as hard as possible to make sure they were closed. The stem was tight against the valve, but it continued to drip. I had to do something. I couldn't be driving down the road, leaking sewage.

One of the exits should have a campground. They'll know where an RV repair shop is.

About twenty-five miles to the north, I saw a KOA sign. By the time I saw the exit for the KOA, I couldn't get to it safely. The next exit put me back on a narrow tree-shrouded road. There I sat, wondering what to do. In spite of my trips through the Kentucky woods, I usually didn't get lost. Ah, well . . .

I reasoned that without a navigator, I had to memorize my route. Sure it was hard job. A wrong maneuver would put me exactly where I sat.

Now what? It's impossible to tell if the road ends down there or if it goes on to get me into more trouble.

As I glanced in my side mirror, a car pulled in next to me. The man scrunched down in his seat so I could see him and asked, "Are you lost?"

"Yes, I sure am. I'm looking for the KOA. I missed the turn."

"You did. Follow me and I'll take you over there."

"Gee, thanks! That's awfully nice of you."

His wife smiled at me as she held her little white poodle on her lap. "It's really not a bother. We used to have a motor home and know all the things that can go wrong."

As I pulled the camper to the side of the road at the KOA, I got out to thank them.

"You'll be OK now," he said. "It's a nice KOA. They'll be able to help you with whatever you need."

"The fact is I really need an RV repair shop. I'm sure they'll know where there is one."

"Why, what's wrong?"

"My black water is leaking."

"Oh…say, there's an empty field a couple miles down the road. Just follow me and I'll see if I can help you. When you get to the lot, pull in a ways, so that you are far enough off the road."

Flabbergasted by his willingness to work on a strange woman's black water valve, I agreed without a question. As I approached the field, I could see that the entrance was sandy. I stopped. "Don't worry, you won't get stuck," he yelled.

I stepped on the accelerator to decrease that possibility and kept going until I reached a high, dry area.

For the life of me, I didn't know what this fellow intended to do that I hadn't already done. I gave him the key and he unlocked the bin. He pushed, banged and shoved on the valve and stem.

"There must be something stuck in there. How full is your black water?"

"There's not much in it. I emptied both tanks this morning."

Before I could say another word, he had the safety cap off. Sewage spilled onto his hands.

I gasped, "Oh no! Quick, wash your hands, so you don't get sick."

I ran to the bin that housed the fresh water and opened the valve so the water would run out. "I'll get some soap and rags. I'll be right back."

In less than a second, he pulled the stem out for the black water and the remainder of the sewage spilled onto the ground. Words didn't come.

Looking at me from his hunched position, he said, "Don't worry, if this is the worst thing that happens to me in my lifetime, I'll be pretty lucky."

219

Carolee O'Neill

By the time I got back with the rags and the soap, I saw that he had rinsed his hand and was using a handkerchief to wipe them.

"I think you'll be OK now. Just watch it. As soon as you get home take it in to have it checked."

Overwhelmed by his gesture, I never asked his name. He refused payment. What would a person offer for such a deed? Maybe someday this gracious man and his wife will read this book. Then they will know that I wished I would've hugged them. I wished I would've shed some tears to show them my appreciation. After they saw me safely on the road, I could only say a prayer of thanksgiving for another couple of eagles of the highest caliber.

Driving through the gates of the Horse Farm outside of Lexington, overcast skies gave way to a misty cool rain. The desk clerk waved his hand toward the campground, "Just take any spot. I'll collect from you later." The campsites weren't level and there wasn't a sewer hookup. That dampened my spirits. With the recent experience with the black water valve, I had to have a sewer connection. I couldn't be sure the valve wouldn't leak, and I couldn't go without a bathroom. If the skies cleared going north, I would be home by at least nine that evening.

As soon as I could, I had the rig at a service center close to my home. Now being an expert in the black water department the hard way, I spoke to the manager.

"I want you to take the electric valve off the camper and replace it with a manual valve. The electric one hasn't worked right since I had the first tire separation. It must have taken a whack when that happened as the bottom of the bin is bowed upwards. It shouldn't take long to do that. There are four screws that have to come out to get it off. Then just clip the wires and cap them. I know a valve is about twenty dollars."

A week later, I went to pick up the coach. I stood gawking at a bill for $200. "Where's the manager? I'm not paying this. I told you what to do and it doesn't take two hours to replace a manual valve, more like fifteen minutes."

The secretary stammered as she said, "I'll get the mechanic and ask him what he did to the coach."

"And what's this extra forty dollars for?"

"Oh, you had a flat tire and we had to pump it up."

Thunderstruck, I gasped, "You charged me forty dollars to put air in a tire?"

"I'm sure there had to be more to it than that."

When the mechanic showed up, my attitude had regained its composure somewhat but sprang to my boiling point, anyway.

This better be good.

"Well, I spent two hours on it, trying to save the electric mechanism for you."

"It was done for.

It couldn't be fixed." I shouted in amazement.

"Inside the electric housing is a valve just like the manual one. I left specific instructions on what I wanted done."

He repeated himself.

He spent two hours at eighty dollars an hour to repair something that couldn't be fixed.

They had my keys and wouldn't give them back until I paid the bill. Looks like I'd be writing another letter to the Better Business Bureau and to the Attorney General's Office.

Instead, I asked for a letter from the company that stated the electric valve had been damaged by the tire separation. That might help me collect from ABC.

Home felt good but in spite of all the interesting mishaps, I set my mind on my next adventure.

California, here I come.

Chapter 36

California would be a long drive alone. The possibility of a breakdown increased with each passing mile. Two trips to Florida, one to the east coast and another to Washington State, put the odometer close to twenty-three thousand miles. As the coach was well maintained, there wasn't a particular concern that something would happen.

I studied the road atlas and considered the locations of things like truck stops and rest areas.

Having made a few trips to Hawaii, I had grown to love the power of the azure waters of the Pacific and the surf smashing against the black lava rock.

On my way south, I'd stop for a brief visit and see my brother Tom. I'd then cut across Oklahoma on 44 and take the southern route to avoid as much altitude as possible. With many miles between towns and gas stations, I wouldn't wait for my tank to register empty, like David did. He'd drive until his warning light came on, and then grumble because he couldn't find a diesel station. With a half empty tank, I'd be looking for a station.

The rest of the trip held few eventful, except for a good case of the flu and another bout with altitude sickness as I climbed over five thousand feet going through Texas Canyon on I-10. Not being in a hurry, I could recover for a week at the Voyageur Campground outside of Tucson. I'd visit some old friends, ride my bike and maybe run into some of the fellows that taught me about motor homes.

223

Wouldn't they be surprised that I actually bought one?

Although I made new friends, my old ones were on the road. That's why they bought motor homes.

Traveling west, I could swear that I could smell the salt water. My imagination had already landed on the beach. Before I did that, I'd be spending Christmas with my nephew's family, Chuck, Pam, his wife, Steve and Rob's family.

With great anticipation, I listened to their Christmas plans. Pam and I shopped for the grandchildren in specialty stores and had some unique lunches. As we wrapped gifts, we listened as Steve, an accomplished pianist, gave us a Christmas concert. On Christmas Eve, before we opened gifts, we sat with the lights dimmed while Chuck read the story of our Father's most precious gift to us, the Christ Child. Tears filled my eyes as the words softened my heart.

The true gift of giving was revealed once again. Christmas morning we went to a church service in a private home where we broke bread and took of the wine in remembrance of His gifts to us. The celebration continued with the serving of a delicious meal. Being part of this group that shared the word of God and fellowship made it a memorable Christmas, one I would never forget.

Sunlight streamed through the tall timbers that lined the narrow road as I drove through the "Valley of the Giants" in California. The velvety moss on the boulders captured the brilliance of the light, reflecting it throughout the thick undergrowth.

The hills, curves and valleys of highway 101 refreshed my tired soul as they presented their anticipated beauty.

Continuing toward the northern shores of California, heavy rains drenched the forest all the way to the Arcata, Oregon coastline. Giving up on the sun, I parked in an empty lot to sit out the storm. By the next morning, a cool haze hung low over the ocean, making the rain seem endless. Turning back would be the best thing to do.

Instead of taking the same road through the "Valley of the Giants", I took the bypass on highway 101. It wasn't much better than the narrow road through the giants, except this time the redwoods were deeper and the evergreens more pronounced. After two days of keeping the motor home on its side of the narrow, winding road, and stopping to enjoy the beauty, I wanted to have someplace to call home.

Beverlee, my high school buddy, lived in Mendocino. There I could get some rest. Reaching highway 20, my turnoff, I was relieved to see a sign that read, "Mendocino 30 miles."

It's a good thing I'm almost there, because I'm beat. The campground should be easy to find. Beverlee's place looks like it's right off the main street of Mendocino. I've made my way across the country; I can make it the rest of the way.

Ahead lay a straightaway that looked like I could glide to town in a breeze. After a mile or two of relaxation, the road took a sharp turn to the right, and then a quick left. It became a zigzag trail that

climbed and descended too fast for a tired driver. I
was back to sheared cliffs with nothing but a
skimpy guardrail for protection; at least it wasn't
sand. This time, I faced plenty of traffic. Somehow,
my adrenals kicked in to awaken my awareness.
After too much time twisting and turning to the
whims of a road, I glanced at the clock on the dash.

*I've been at this for over an hour and I still
have five miles to go.*

Two miles from the ocean, the road
straightened, and it started to rain. I didn't care. My
insides cheered. The ocean was a breath away.

A private tour, given to me by my friend
Beverlee, included Mendocino's history, being
treated to gourmet restaurants, driving route One,
touring unusual spots like a blow-hole, and my
favorite—being shown how her cookie factory
worked.

In my spare time, which wasn't much, I
fretted about the drive back to highway 101, a total
waste of time and energy. I must have been in bad
shape on the way in because driving out left me
wondering what I was doing on the way in. Of
course, being on the inside put me against the
mountain instead of looking down a steep cliff. I
had plenty of miles ahead of me yet if I wasted to
go all the way to San Diego. I needed to shape up
my attitude.

Monterey would be one of my first stops. I
wouldn't miss it for the world. However, I found it
difficult to find an acceptable campground in the
area. After finding one, the hard-nosed owner told

me to go into a campsite that had a sharp upward angle. I told him I couldn't get into it because my backend was slung too low. He insisted that he could coach me into the spot. After several back and forth angular motions, the coach got up the hill and in its spot. It seemed strange that the backend registered few complaints. It usually made more noise going in or out of a gas station. Something had to be wrong. The answer came when I saw the nylon fibers peeled off the back brush. It had folded under the coach and acted as a buffer between the coach and the pavement.

Grumbling about the brush, I heard a rap on my screen door while I prepared supper.

"Hello there, neighbor," Bill said. "We just pulled in with our fifth wheel and thought we'd stop over and visit with you folks for a bit."

I looked down into the smiling faces of two seniors. "There's only me, but I'd love to visit with you."

"You're alone?" Jennie asked as I offered her a chair.

"Sure am."

"Good for you," Bill said. "We ran into another gal about six months ago, didn't we, Jen? She was traveling by herself too. Don't see very many of them though, and they're all younger than you."

"Do you know anyone in California?" Jen asked.

"Not out this way. I do have some relatives in Sacramento, but that's pretty much it."

Carolee O'Neill

"Well, we live a little north of here. We're up here for a bit to enjoy the ocean. I'll give you our phone number and home address so you'll have someone to call if you have a problem."

"Gee! That's really nice of you."

The word gracious came to mind, when I thought about Jen and Bill's actions. We shared our days and the idiosyncrasies of owning an RV. That's when I told him about the damage to my back brush. Bill decided to take a look.

"They're pretty inexpensive and, frankly, I don't think they work that well. They're not worth making a stink over, that's for sure. It's pretty hard to get a campsite around Monterey, so just chalk it up to experience."

After exploring the beauty of the area for a week, the time had come to get the camper out of the site. I had to angle it like I did to back it in, only this time with no help. Using small back and forth motions, I hooked the backend of the camper onto something that didn't want to move. I rushed to see what had happened.

How in the world did I manage that?

Hung up on the retaining wall, my blood ran cold and my heart got another good workout. I ran back to the cab, hoping to pull the unit free. Not complaining about the back brush had turned out to be a good thing after all.

I wiggled into another angular position and ended up taking down the wall on the opposite side. After some long moments of shifting back and forth to release my backend, I finally got the camper out of the site and on to level ground. I do believe the racket from tumbling walls caught Bill's attention.

"What happened?"

"I tried to get out of my space and got caught on them. Now what am I going to do?"

"You couldn't have taken both of them down, that's not possible. There's no way you could have gotten the camper in that kind of a position. I think somebody else did the other one."

Little does he know!

"I better call Bob, my insurance agent. I've done some property damage."

"No, I wouldn't do that. Let me take a closer look."

"I'm pretty sure I did them both, Bill."

"Look at them! They're a mess. It's pretty obvious that other RV's have hit them and that they've been put back up again. I wouldn't worry about it. They've asked for it, the way these sites are built. Is the motor home OK?"

"I don't know. I haven't thought that far ahead. I'm still suffering from the retaining walls. I'm not sure I would know what to look for anyway."

"Don't worry, Jen and I will check underneath to make sure you're OK."

How could I have done something so stupid? Guess I'm getting good at it.

"Everything looks good," Bill said. "You'll be OK. I'll go tell the maintenance man what happened while you relax for a minute and get your bearings."

When Bill told the maintenance man what had happened, he said, "Everyday somebody takes them down and every day I put them back up again."

Needless to say, relief flooded my innards.

Jen and Bill waved as I drove out of the campground. "Drive careful now," Bill hollered. "And don't hit any more retaining walls."

Every chance possible, I watched a sunset along the ocean, each with its own personality, none a disappointment. The marriage of a sunset and the azure waters of the Pacific allowed a person to glimpse God's splendor. His paintbrush melded the colors into an everlasting union, thrusting them outward to show a hint of His glory. Standing on the boardwalk in Lahaina, Hawaii, a person could get an unabridged view every evening of this splendor.

As I parked along the Monterey coast, I took care not to get too close. High places give me the heebie-jeebies, especially after we took that "unpleasant" Apache Lake drive.

The walk through the bamboo forest on our way to see Akaka Falls, on the island of Hawaii, took second place. All of a sudden, the foliage opened to the thunderous roar of rushing waters, as though somebody had pulled a curtain.

The ground became my savior as I went face down, dug my nails into the dirt, and became an immovable object. David ran to the railing, climbed over (almost stepping on my fingers), and began taking pictures. From my prone position, I screamed at David to come back before he fell. He turned, looked at me, laughed and continued to click. From this vantage point, it would be safe to say that the splendor of the falls eluded me.

I had arrived early at my special spot on the Monterey coastline. I didn't want anyone or anything to interfere with the myriad of colors that would move stealthily across the horizon. Perched on the top of the cliff in the Honda, I waited for the show to begin.

The seats in the back of the car had been folded to allow room for my bike. Because of this, I couldn't move my seat back any further. Feeling cramped, I shifted my weight.

The ground on the ocean side of the car crumpled.

The car dipped sideways.

My once calm demeanor had done a jump-start everywhere: my body trembled, my face flushed hot, my pulse rate banged to all points north and south.

I screamed, "Dear God! I'm doomed."

The Honda tipped again.

The sound of rolling stones and gravel warned of my impending flight, bouncing off the rugged edges of the cliff to my demise.

Afraid to move, I started to pray. This time it was an act of contrition. *Oh my God, forgive me for having offended You. I ask it in Jesus' precious name.*

In a flash, God answered, "You've got four-wheel drive, remember? That's the gear you thought you'd never use!"

Oh yes—I do! I forgot!

I shifted the gears. The tires spun as rocks shot like bullets from beneath them. My innards cheered as the Honda propelled itself onto terra firma, just like David's truck.

Did I see the sunset?

I think so. However, I do believe that the horrifying thought of tumbling into eternity might have diluted my memory of it. The gear that I told John I never wanted had my complete appreciation.

As I gathered my thoughts and prepared to leave Monterey, Carmel, Point Lobos and Big Sur—what could I say? Where does one go after nature provides perfection?

Shelves of jutting rock clung to the mammoth cliffs that plunged to the azure waters of the Pacific. Gulls circled the surf as their caws echoed into the distance. Other white sand beaches hid between the darkened rocks as the surf waltzed to the rhythm of the sea. My spirit enchanted, I never wanted to leave; however, life goes on just as it did after David died. This adventure would go forth as well.

The drive down the coast ended at Morro Bay, for a month with a sewage treatment plant next door. Need I say more?

Just before I was ready to leave, a note reached me from a friend from Indiana. Mary Jane now lived in Carpentaria, California, and had re-married a few months ago. A few days later, she stood on my doorstep, smiling her best elfish grin. Like silly little girls, we talked for hours, giggled repeatedly and hugged often.

I could park in a vacant lot close to them or else at the state park nearby. As positioning the camper in the lot didn't work, I headed for the state park. Without a prior reservation, I had to take what was available.

A heavy rainfall that lasted for almost a week, left the camper's tires sitting in water halfway up their rims my first night. That situation wouldn't do. The next morning, I got a spot right across from the ocean.

How lucky could I get?

To make sure that I didn't forget how cold and damp California winters could be, the drizzle and intermittent rain reminded me the day before I left.

A little rain, I didn't consider a big deal. I loved the sound of rain on the roof, especially since I had the roof fixed. As long as things stayed sensible, I loved it.

I remember David looking out of our seventh floor window in Maui when sirens began to blare.

"I wonder what they're for?" he asked.

I hurried to the balcony, seeing palm trees sweeping the ground and the ocean boiling a sandy color beyond the breakers.

I yelled, "We're in the middle of a tropical storm. We're supposed to evacuate."

The wind whipped water against the sides of the camper, bringing me back to reality. Things were not going to stay sensible. The storm had gone from a soothing pitter-patter to a furious attack.

Carolee O'Neill

With the ocean steps away, I expected to be airborne very soon, and not surviving.

Back and forth the coach veered. Tents collapsed and debris flew through the air.

The storms power came from a vacant lot on my left. The campers parked on my right gained only a smidgeon of protection from my coach.

I told God that if these were my last moments on earth to make it quick.

After several minutes of shaking, I figured I couldn't do anything about the obvious danger so I decided to go to bed. At least I'd be laying down when I died.

I went to close the blind in the bedroom to block the frightening scene and found the counter full of water. The box of Kleenex sitting on the sill had done a pretty good job of soaking some of it up, until I picked it up. The water ran out of it, like a bucket with a hole. I gathered as many rags as possible, trying to keep ahead of the water.

By morning, the storm had convinced me that it might not be the best idea to be so close to the ocean.

With the dawn came the day of departure. Giving Mary Jane and Don one last hug, a tearful smile disclosed the memories we created.

Now I'd have to get the coach ready for travel. Having taken a good beating, I asked Dave, a young fellow in the campground, to check my turn signals, brake and taillights before I took off.

"No," he kept yelling. "They aren't lighting."

234

Not one lit to cover my behind. Dan began checking fuses and wires to see if he could locate the problem. Of course, that brought every fellow in the campground over for a look and a comment. After an hour, Dan at least got the signals to work with the car. Later, road service checked the lights and told me that the storm had forced salt water into all the housings. As soon as I turned on the lights, the water blew out all the bulbs.

Thank heaven it was a simple problem. Or was it? Now I had salt water eating away at my wiring and a window that leaked.

Chapter 37

Standing on the pier in San Diego, I gazed across the clear, sapphire waters that would always be engraved in my mind. In the panoramic view of the shoreline, I could see bikers swerve in and around people as they dashed to their miles of nowhere. In the midst of the confusion, it seemed strange to see men and women in yoga positions, practicing meditation. Other enthusiasts' power walked along the boardwalk, carrying weights to increase their endurance and muscle mass.

The southern shoreline of San Diego boasted sandy beaches with fewer cliffs than the northern coastline. Although it was my favorite city, the beauty of highway one had captured my essence. The drive from Monterey to Morro Bay, which I did three times, created memories of foaming waters that reached skyward after smashing against the darkened rocks. Pebbles tumbled. Shells and sand united to follow the command of the riptides only to be pushed inward with the next surge of power. When the winds of strength calmed, the waters rolled to the shore, never revealing their turbulent undertow.

Eons of time will someday smooth the jagged rocks and steal their harshness, like some people mellow with age. A wise person probably would've stayed home. That would've been a mistake.

I'll never forget the surprised look on the faces of people in cars stopped at lights when I swung the motor home for a wide right turn. Their faces showed concern, but I knew I had plenty of room. As soon as I cleared their vehicles, I got the thumbs up sign and a memory bank full of grins. Staying home would have filled my years with the redundancies of life, not grins. Seizing the moments was the right thing to do.

The time I spent along the coast had fled too quickly. Regardless, the blessings remained. Now, before I turn homeward, I'll have to be content with one last sunset provided by my heavenly Father.

Deepened shades of burnt orange touched the heavens and the earth as light descended beneath the horizon. Staring at the fading sunset, the words of my elderly patient came to mind, "God certainly has a beautiful way of saying good morning." With an astoundingly beautiful vision before me, I'd have to say He had a pretty spectacular way of saying goodnight. Without a doubt, God planned this journey so I would grow closer to His heart and challenge others to go forth in faith.

Carolee O'Neill

Epilog

For six years, I managed to avoid the grieving process in spite of the dark hole that radiated emptiness in my being. The daily challenges with the motor home kept me too busy to grieve the loss of my loved one. Yet, nature had the final word. I became severely crippled with arthritis. I feared surgery. A long list of drug reactions reminded me I wasn't a good candidate. I procrastinated, yet continued to pray for an answer.

Then I remembered that God never gives us more than we can handle nor fails to provide a way out. Maybe surgery was my way out.

Again, fear overpowered my thoughts. I had been blessed with a good primary care physician when I moved to Wisconsin, but would I have the same luck with a surgeon. Considering this, I temporarily escaped surgery by rationalizing that perhaps God wanted me in a wheelchair to do His work. Then the pain overpowered the fear as my condition continued to deteriorate. I was forced to see my doctor. My primary physician ordered x-rays to confirm her suspicions.

"There's nothing left of your hip joints. No wonder you're in so much pain. I know a surgeon that I'd like you to interview."

I trembled at the thought.

Seeing my reaction, she added, "If you don't like him, I'll find another one. You don't have to make a decision right now. Let's see what Dr. Terry has to say."

By this time, I had been out of nursing for twenty-some years. Surgery for a total hip replacement had changed somewhat, but not the pain or rehab. The medical library provided me with the latest research that gave me four pages of questions. I intended to be prepared.

To my surprise, Dr. Terry didn't try to convince me to have surgery. Instead, he put his feet up on his desk and answered every question. While he talked I prayed. Should I have this done? By the time the doctor had finished, the options were clear. I either had the surgery or spent the remainder of my life in a wheelchair.

Toward the end of the conversation, Dr. Terry mentioned that he was a Christian. My reaction was, "Yeah sure." A few days later, I learned from a friend that she had Dr. Terry for her knee surgery.

"You're never going to believe this, but he comes to your side before surgery and prays with you," she said.

Sure enough, he did just that. He had the right answers, the bedside manner and the skill to perform these surgeries. God had sent me this incredible surgeon to heal my broken body. I knew I had to proceed with both surgeries.

Three days after the surgery, I went to an immaculate nursing home for rehab, with caring and efficient staff. The hospice wing bordered the convalescent area, so hospice patients would often join us for meals in the main dinner room.

Sitting together, we soon became friends. One day the gal who sat across from me told the group that she had developed an infection in her surgical hip. Something we all feared.

We prayed that the antibiotic would work, but it didn't. The infection spread to her shoulder, putting her back in the hospital to have the prosthesis removed and replaced at a later date. I feared for her life.

The drama played out before me. Hospice patients continued to parade the halls, a huge hospice banner draped above the kitchen counter, the families of hospice patients gathered in the main lounge to hear the morbid news about their loved ones. Their happenings coupled with in my emotions. I started to cry about everything. Nightmares plagued my dreams. The staff became concerned that I was depressed. I argued that I wasn't—I was worried about my friend.

I decided I had to get out of the nursing home no matter what my condition. I couldn't look at the oncology patients without crying: I couldn't watch television without crying, I couldn't think of my friend without crying. The doctor signed the discharge papers and sent me home. That didn't change anything. I continued to cry.

It wasn't until a few weeks had passed that I realized that my friend's infection had triggered my grieving process. I had hidden my pain in that dark hole, but the hospice sign and the hospice patients took me back to the terror that stayed locked in my heart from losing David.

Three months after the first surgery, I had the second hip done by Dr. Terry. The next months my body and my spirit took time to heal. I did this by allowing myself to cry, to talk about David, and to write, "A Reason to Dream" to record many of the memories, like the trip to church on Christmas Eve when David ushered or the vision of him tearing up the kitchen floor. The sight of my Bible reminded me that God would always help me to remember that David was with Him in spirit and with me in my soul—a much better place. God has given me this opportunity so I can do His work, standing straight.

God willing, I will travel with the motor home, hear a Strauss waltz, and play golf just for the fun of it. Moreover, when I go to meet my Maker, I'll be dancing with the angels.

The End

Carolee O'Neill

Excerpt from, "A Reason to Dream.

The Trip

The day finally arrived for my departure. As soon as I closed the garage door I felt a sense of relief. The drive would be a hurried one, and yet relaxing, a change of pace. I hadn't seen Phyllis in a long time, so she was excited about my visit.

Reaching Sterling, Colorado, I began to feel ill. The gradual increase in altitude with the sun bearing down on the driver's side had caught up with me. Seeing a sign for a rest station by the chamber of commerce, I took the exit. The sign posted next to the chamber read four thousand four hundred feet. *I'm surprised the altitude is having such an effect. But then, what did I expect? I haven't given a thought to my own health beyond the constant buzzing in my head.* I reached for my cooler and began eating as much cheese as I could to stabilize my system. After an hour's rest, I felt the protein had done its job. As the rays of the sun were part of the problem, I'd provide some shade for myself before going back on the road. Opening the window on the driver's side, I took a small towel, lapped it over the top edge and closed the window. Now I had some shade and I could see the traffic through my side mirror. From that point on I took it easy. I didn't want to be worn out when I arrived in Colorado Springs. Knowing Phyllis, she'd have something planned.

242.

I hadn't been at Phyllis's home for more than a few hours when a call came in. Phyllis handed me the phone, saying it was the hospice nurse. My first thought was that Joyce wanted to make sure I had arrived safely.

Then I heard her say, "David is very bad. We don't expect him to last through the night. We've hired a private duty nurse to stay with him until you get back."

Standing became difficult. Cold chills ran through my body.

My reply was grief-stricken, but strong. "Where do you think I am, next door? I could never get there in time. Why didn't you use my respite instead of hiring a nurse?"

"We couldn't. He refuses to leave the house."

Phyllis stood close, asking, "What is it?"

I muttered, "David is dying."

I don't remember hanging up the phone. Frantically, I began grabbing my belongings from the closet and the dresser. Unable to concentrate, I couldn't remember what I had brought or where I had put things. Many items had already been dispersed into other areas of the home, like the bathroom and the kitchen. I fretted that I'd leave something behind. My mind wouldn't remember. It was a blank to worldly possessions.

"You can't leave!" Phyllis pleaded. "It's too dangerous to be on the road in your condition. Please don't do this."

"I have to! I have to get back. Somehow the good Lord will get me there. Please don't worry. I'll be OK. I promise that before I leave, I'll do a meditation. Right now, I have to get the car packed."

Minutes later the phone rang again. I felt a scream mounting in my throat, had David died? I shook my head "no" as Phyllis handed me the phone. Her eyes saddened. Gloom was written on her face.

My voice sounded hollow when I said, "Hello."

It was Joyce. "I don't want you so upset that you can't drive. He's not that bad."

"What?" I gasped.

"You need to come back anyway because he's not allowing us to care for him."

Shocked by the callousness of the first call, I said, "How could you do this to me? I can barely stand up. Did you even consider what kind of an effect this would have on me? You should have thought of that before you told me he was dying. I gave you the authority to put him in respite. Are you telling me you can't do that?"

"Yes."

"With David's history of bullheadedness, you didn't know he could refuse your orders before I left? You didn't know this was a possibility? You should have known this! You should have known what to do if it happened. But it appears you don't know your own administrative policy, do you? How could you let me drive all this way for nothing?"

"I'm sorry, but we never expected him to refuse the care. None of that matters now. It's water over the dam. As you drive back, we are asking that

244.

you stop and let us know where you are."

My heart fluttered and pounded in my chest as I listened to the flat monotone in which she delivered her demands. The receiver shook in my hand; I raised my left hand to steady it. I wanted to run away. I didn't want to talk to her any more. Nothing made sense. I felt the bed for a place to sit, but it was covered with suitcases.

"I have a hearing loss, remember? You want me to waste time looking for a phone I can understand on, so you will know where I am, for what? What will that accomplish? I have to pack to leave, goodbye."

Phyllis had done her best to gather my things. Again, she begged me not to leave.

"There's nothing you can do. There's no sense killing yourself over this. You have given hospice all the authority they need to handle any situation."

"I know, but it doesn't look like they plan to use it. The nurse said we would have to pay for the private duty nurse, and that'll be a lot. I'll have to leave, whether or not I want to. I'm sorry it didn't work out."

Before leaving I sat very still in a comfortable chair and closed my eyes. After a few deep breaths I imagined the azure water of the Pacific. My heart slowly returned to its normal rhythm, but the ordeal left me weak. *Perhaps I'll begin to feel better once I'm out of the altitude.*

The duty hospice imposed upon me caused me to worry about David's future care. I didn't know what would happen if I didn't follow the rules. Maybe I was being paranoid, but I couldn't chance it. I'd have to do as I was told.

On the way I stopped a couple of times, but I couldn't find a phone. It wasn't until I reached the motel at two-thirty in the morning that I was able to call.

Upon getting the nurse, I asked, "Is David in respiratory distress?"

After a pause she replied, "I don't know."
"You don't know?"

"Well, I don't have anything to compare it with. I don't know how he was before I got here."

"What!" I snapped. "I'm asking you if he is having trouble breathing."

"No…I don't think so."

"Are you a registered nurse?"

"Yes."

"Then go in and check him. I want to know his condition."

She returned to tell me that he was resting comfortably, a pat nursing response.

"Would you please let hospice know that I'm in Illinois? I should be home sometime late afternoon or early evening."

"I can't. They're not open now; and I go off duty at six this morning."

"Then ask the nurse coming on duty to call them."

"I can tell her, but I can't guarantee she'll call them."

After hanging up, my mind continued to do reruns of the conversation. I was tired, maybe she misunderstood.

How could a nurse not know how to answer a question on respiratory distress? Couldn't a layperson answer that one?

Being beyond exhaustion, I couldn't sleep. The cruelty of the first phone conversation with the hospice nurse overwhelmed my thoughts. Unrelated thoughts jumped the fence of logic.

Did the nurse color the truth when she called back? Would David be gone by the time I returned? I bet she changed her story to calm me down, so I wouldn't have an accident. Then they wouldn't be responsible. Could I possibly make it back in time? If I fall asleep I won't get an early start. Then I'll miss him forever.

Carolee O'Neill

Appendixes

Things I Learned.

1. Being afraid is not an excuse for not doing something.
2. Awnings go up and down in <u>four easy to remember steps.</u>
3. Most mechanics on a coach have a reset button.
4. There should be a reset button on all technicians.
5. Like the rest of us, technicians know about half of what you think they do.
6. When you are driving a rig alone, the hardest thing to do is to blow your nose.
7. The next hardest thing is to take a splinter out of your prominent finger or hand.
8. Flying J Truck stops have the best glazed donuts.
9. Most technicians think they have the answer before you ask the question.
10. There are many more eagles in the world than there are turkeys.
11. I'll never get tired of looking at the azure waters of the Pacific.
12. There's always someone who is willing to help.
13. Always pull the driver's seat all the way forward before bringing the slide in, unless you want to peel the leather off the back of the driver's seat.
14. Ice cube trays are not a worthy opponent against a slide-out that's coming in.
15. The noise from a vibrator slamming against steel will leave a lasting impression.

16. Wire frames used for toasting bread on a gas stove don't work very well.
17. Coastal Highway One in California should be traveled more than once in a lifetime.
18. When you've lost your hearing aid the first place to look for it is in your ear.
19. There are no truck stops along Highway One in California that I saw, anyway. Thank heaven.
20. After two years with your RV you'll have most of the bugs out, but maybe not the ants.
21. Don't fill the battery cells too close to the top. The acid will overflow when you put the caps back on and will eat the tray holding the batteries.
22. Don't allow your gray water tank to fill up before you empty it. The water will back up into the shower, putting pressure on the drain. If you have a small hole in the drain caulking, you'll get water under your shower = mold.
23. Great Clips gives a good haircut at a very reasonable price.
24. Key Lime pie is best when it's made with real key limes.
25. The best Key Lime pie is found in the Keys or on Sanibel. Yummy!
26. You can get drunk tasting wine as you drive through California.
27. Everything is easy if you know how to do it.
28. A person can manage very well with a lot less than she think she can.
29. Cell phones are a royal pain.
30. Gauges for the holding tanks are seldom accurate.

31. A small ceramic space heater runs on 15 amps as long as nothing else is running.

32. Gas stoves don't use a lot of propane.

33. There's a book called, "The Next Exit" that outlines everything that exit offers. The book is less expensive than the latest technology.

34. RVers don't always know what they are talking about. Go to the Book/Manual.

35. I am now an Introverted Extrovert.

36. There are wonderful hidden places to explore like Aqua Caliente Park in the Tanque Verde area around Tucson, Arizona.

37. Sometimes I have a tendency to expect God to do it all without me.

38. Dry camping taught me how valuable water is and how to conserve it.

39. With a hearing loss it's easier to deal with strangers than it is with those you know. Strangers only have to put up with you for a short time.

40. Loneliness can become a problem only if you let it. Remember, the world is your neighbor.

41. I'm very comfortable with silence.

42. I've been told that I'm a gutsy lady.

43. People who pull their car up to get gas behind a motor home have no idea how long their wait is going to be.

44. Everything that goes wrong is not an emergency.

45. Veggie Pizza and a Chocolate Malt at Appleby's are the best.

46. Traveling when Monarch butterflies are migrating will get you an orange motor home.

47. I'm a lot more humble.

48. Going to the company that made your unit isn't always a guarantee that you'll get the right answers.
49. If you ask enough questions and go to enough dealerships, after three years you'll have most of the correct answers.
50. When the refrigerator dies you can always rely on a bag of ice.
51. Young deplore traffic. The elderly are starved for movement and sound.
52. It's a good idea to stay in a campground unless you are a glutton for punishment.
53. Elephant seals desert their young on the beach as soon as they breed with papa seal. Hmm!
54. If you want to give your kids fits, tell them that you picked up a hitch-hiker.
55. When asked how I can drive such a big rig I reply, "I just get the front there and the rest follows."
56. Hang on tight to the sewer hose when you disconnect or it will vanish into the cleanout sewer.
57. It's not uncommon for men to give me the thumbs up sign, as well as women.
58. Don't talk about what it is like to walk a mile in someone else's shoes unless you can retrace their steps in an old pair of their worn-out shoes.
59. I was told that I could get in trouble sitting in a chair.
60. After all this, God needs a vacation.

Appendix 1: Want List for Motor Home/RV

Class C Motor Home-Approximately 28 feet
(Bought 31.5 Ultra Supreme GulfStream)

1. No odors: no smoke/animals or new car smell.
2. Walk around bed.—queen, I might consider two twins, but prefer the queen. No corner bed as they are too hard to make.
3. Slide, need room to do PT exercises.
4. Need dinette for computer.
5. Low mileage.
6. Back up mirror: Yes, if possible.
7. Soft colors, beige, pastels, nothing loud.
8. Lots of storage, inside and out.
9. Passenger chair that swivels. This would be nice. I know it's not always possible.
10. Small enough hump between driver and passenger's seat to be able to get around it easily.
11. No step or small one from cab to unit.
12. Generator—big enough to run the unit and air.
13. Oven-real one, not just convection.
14. No leaks. Has it been maintained to prevent leaks?
15. Test drive until comfortable with instruction on use.
16. Spare tire with necessary jack, etc.
17. Levelers. Some unit have them, you'll have to explain.
18. Stabilizers.
19. Insulation-how much?
20. No soft floor.
21. Does it have an Extended Warranty on Motor? If so, is it transferable?
22. Steps/hand bar/ type.
23. Hitch on back? I'll be taking my bike, maybe pulling a car.
24. Exterior-Fiberglas, don't want alum?
25. Side mirrors that do the job.
26. Central air.

27. Overhead vents.
28. Overhead fan.
29. Make/Model/Year: later model. I understand that the 2003 will be out in July so people should be trading up and it should give me a chance to get a good buy.
30. Entertainment center.
31. Microwave.
32. Well cared for.
33. Large refrig/freezer.
34. Windows in bedroom.
35. Type of bathroom? I plan to use this. I'm not one to go out of the unit for my shower. I don't want a shower that you have to step up and over to get into. In other words, low in front.
36. Are there night/day shades?
37. What kind of wheels does it have?
38. Are there smoke detectors, LP detectors?
39. Do windows open? Broken or cracked? Are there screens and in good condition?
40. Ladder on back?
41. Is the condition of the exterior good or faded?
42. How many batteries and what is the amps/volts/type.
43. Does the motor look like it has been cleaned so as not to show mileage?
44. Are the miles actual miles?
45. Should I consider an extended warranty?
46. Model #, style/ type, motor size.
47. Is there a MSDS sheet on it?
48. Is there a problem with wide body units and being prohibited from going into certain states?
49. Is there a fire extinguisher and has it been tested/refilled?
50. Type of roof.

Appendix 2: Owners Absentee List to Prepare the Home

1. Call Utility Company- put house on vacation. Have water turned off at curb.
2. Cancel or change magazines: AARP, Highways, etc.
3. Inform: American Family, SHHH, Bank, etc.
4. See dentist/doctor.
5. Arrange for mail with post office or Good Sam.
6. Drain pipes and hot water heater in home. PUT HOSE IN DRAIN.
7. Turn everything off. Softener, etc.
8. Turn main off.
9. Call Telephone Company: have phone put on vacation or disconnected depending on length of time I'll be gone.
10. Clean and cover A/C.
11. Cover outside table.
12. Put cords out for heat tapes.
13. Sweep out garage.
14. Winterize sprinkling system.
15. Turn off and unplug dehumidifier.
16. Put bulbs out.
17. Put Hedge Apples out.
18. Turn heat down.
19. Put lamp on timer.
20. Get rid of any plants.
21. Empty and unplug refrigerator.
22. Disconnect hoses and put away.
23. Call Indiana or state for tax form to be forwarded.
24. Bolt on mail box.
25. Change filter on furnace.
26. Check smoke detectors.
27. Take water out of toilet.
28. Trim all plants back in garden.

Appendix 3: Advertisement disclosing Inverter.

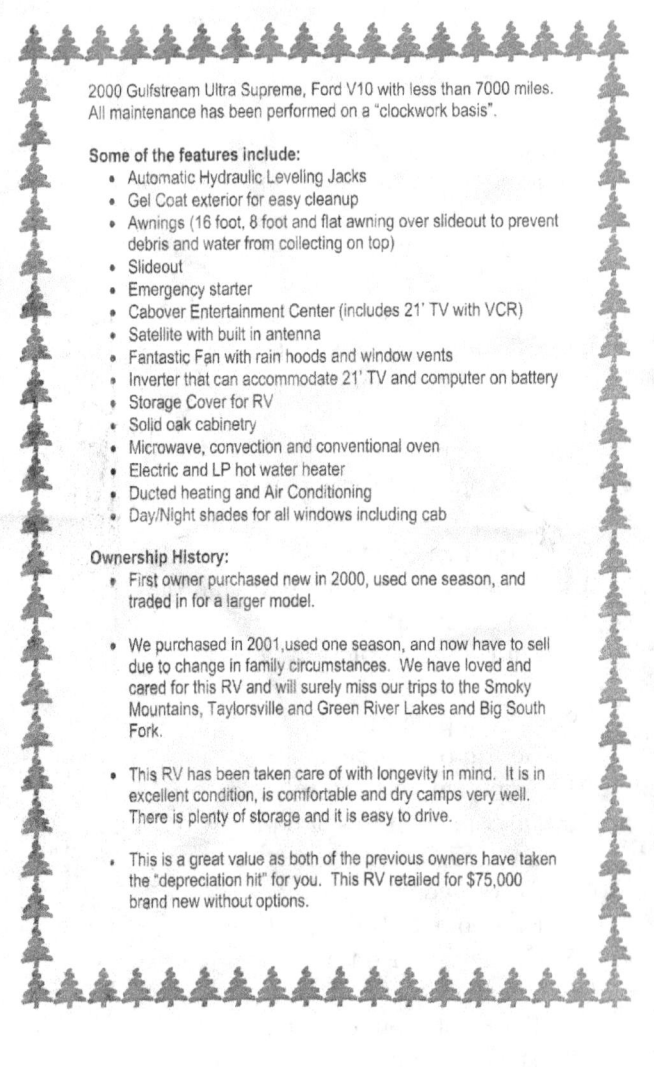

2000 Gulfstream Ultra Supreme, Ford V10 with less than 7000 miles. All maintenance has been performed on a "clockwork basis".

Some of the features include:
- Automatic Hydraulic Leveling Jacks
- Gel Coat exterior for easy cleanup
- Awnings (16 foot, 8 foot and flat awning over slideout to prevent debris and water from collecting on top)
- Slideout
- Emergency starter
- Cabover Entertainment Center (includes 21' TV with VCR)
- Satellite with built in antenna
- Fantastic Fan with rain hoods and window vents
- Inverter that can accommodate 21' TV and computer on battery
- Storage Cover for RV
- Solid oak cabinetry
- Microwave, convection and conventional oven
- Electric and LP hot water heater
- Ducted heating and Air Conditioning
- Day/Night shades for all windows including cab

Ownership History:
- First owner purchased new in 2000, used one season, and traded in for a larger model.

- We purchased in 2001, used one season, and now have to sell due to change in family circumstances. We have loved and cared for this RV and will surely miss our trips to the Smoky Mountains, Taylorsville and Green River Lakes and Big South Fork.

- This RV has been taken care of with longevity in mind. It is in excellent condition, is comfortable and dry camps very well. There is plenty of storage and it is easy to drive.

- This is a great value as both of the previous owners have taken the "depreciation hit" for you. This RV retailed for $75,000 brand new without options.

Appendix 4: Pre-Delivery Inspection-Used.

PRE-DELIVERY INSPECTION-USED

WATER SYSTEM

___ Fresh water fill
___ Fresh water tank
___ Water pump
___ City water conn.
___ All water lines
___ All faucets
___ Water heater
___ Toilet
___ Traps & drain lines
___ Drains & plugs
___ Holding tanks
___ Gate valves
___ Winterize

110 VOLT ELECTIRCAL

___ 110V Sys (Land cord)
___ 110V Recepts
___ GFI Breaker
___ Roof AC Operation
___ Refrigerator Operation
___ Microwave operation
___ Ice maker oper
___ Washer & dryer oper
___ TV Operation
___ VCR Operation
___ TV Antenna Operation
___ Generator oil level
___ Gen. oper. 110 power
___ 110V Water heater

LP SYSTEM

___ LP Tanks
___ Regulator (Dual stage)
___ Gas lines
___ LPG Test 9" wc for
___ 15 minutes
___ Furnace
___ Range
___ Water heater
___ Refrigerator
___ LP Detector

12 VOLT SYSTEM

___ Battery poer oper.
___ Converter oper.
___ 12V Refrig oper
___ Interior lights
___ Radio & tape player

GENERAL APPEARANCE ITEMS

___ 2 sets door & comp keys
___ Awning operation
___ Fire extinguisher

CHASSIS

___ Engine oil
___ All fluid levels
___ Belts & hoses
___ Exterior lights
___ Wipers & washers
___ Tire pressure___ Spare___
___ Lug nuts
___ Break away switch
___ Safety chains
___ Dealer road test
___ Steering adequate
___ Brake performance
___ Speedometer & gauges
___ Cruise control
___ AC & Water heater oper.
___ Elec. or hyd. jacks

ORIENTATION

___ Familiarize owner w/coupling
    and uncoupling
___ Demonstrate all appliances
    and accessories
___ Explain LP Safety

Document: taken from the original developed by dealership.

Appendix 5: INSIDE CHECK LIST FOR RV
1. Appliances off as appropriate.
2. Countertops cleared.
3. Antenna/satellite dish down and booster switch off.
4. Cabinets latched shut.
5. Ceiling vents down.
6. Closet doors closed.
7. Things out from around slide moved before slide brought in.
8. Slide clear to move in or out inside and outside.
9. Drawers closed.
10. Entry doors locked.
11. Step up.
12. Furnace/air conditioner off.
13. Microwave off, door latched.
14. Nightstands bare.
15. Pocket doors secured.
16. Privacy curtain tied back.
17. Refrigerator off as appropriate/ door latched. Has it converted to gas/electric?
18. Refrigerator contents secured.
19. Shelves secure.
20. Shower soap put away.
21. Sink covers in place.
22. Sink drain plugs open.
23. Slide out in/out.
24. Stove burners and oven off/lid down.
25. Toilet seat down.
26. Wall hangings secure.
27. Water heater off.
28. Water pump off.
29. Windows latched.
30. Window blinds down.
31. Water stored in braced position as well as computer, etc.

Appendix 6: OUTSIDE CHECK LIST FOR RV
1. Antenna down/Satellite pointed towards back of coach.
2. Awnings secured/locked.
3. Compartment doors locked.
4. Door mat stored.
5. Doors locked.
6. Gray/Black water emptied as appropriate.
7. Dump valves closed/cap in place and secure.
8. Electric, cable/accessories stowed.
9. Engine checked: oil, belts, fluids, etc.
10. Hood latched.
11. Fresh water tank filled. Needs to be chlorinated first. I take only enough for the toilet.
12. Grab bar closed and secured/safety chain attached.
13. Ladder stowed.
14. Jacks up.
15. EMERGENCY Brake. Shift gear before releasing emergency brake. After travel: release emergency brake and then shift in to park.
16. License plates secure.
17. Lights tested: back up, turn signals, etc.
18. Name plaque stowed.
19. Propane turned off when appropriate.
20. Roof clear.
21. Spare tire checked before each trip.
22. Step raised.
23. Tires checked/pressure. Valves checked-caps tight.
24. Mirrors adjusted.
25. Water hose/regulator, filters, etc. stowed.
26. Wheel covers stowed.
27. Antenna down/Satellite pointed towards back of coach.
28. Awnings secured/locked.
29. Compartment doors locked.
30. Door mat stored.

31. Doors locked.
32. Gray/Black water emptied as appropriate.
33. Dump valves closed/cap in place and secure.
34. Electric, cable/accessories stowed.
35. Engine checked: oil, belts, fluids, etc.
36. Hood latched.
37. Bottled water for drinking.
38. Grab bar closed and secured/safety chain attached.
39. Ladder Stowed.
40. EMERGENCY Brake. Shift gear before releasing emergency brake. After travel: Release emergency brake and then shift in to Park.
41. License plates secure.
42. Lights tested: back up, turn signals, etc.
43. Name plaque stowed.
44. Propane turned off when appropriate.
45. Roof clear.
46. Spare tire checked before each trip.
47. Step raised.
48. Tires checked/pressure. Valves checked-caps tight.
49. Mirrors adjusted.
50. Water hose/regulator, filters, etc. stowed.
51. Wheel covers stowed.
52. Jacks up.

**Inside and Outside Checklist has been developed using "Good Sam" magazine.

Appendix: 7: Dealership: RV Questions/Repairs
Questions:
1.Stove: Is there a vent that needs to be opened and
closed? _____

    If so how?
    How do you adjust a yellow flame?
2. How do you get vent screens out for cleaning?
3. Does the pump need to be turned off during the
day/night when not in use?
4. Are marks on wallpaper from moisture? (From
previous owner.)
5. Is there a light in the refrigerator? (Can't find it.)
6. Holding tanks: Should I use an enzyme in the gray
water tank as well as the black?

    Can testers for tanks be adjusted? _____ If
so, how?
    Hose connector to rinse tank is leaking.
_____

7. What are drains for? 1 is for fresh water? The rest are
for what?

_____

8. Do I only use the bypass valve when winterizing?
Otherwise, always use unit on normal flow?

_____

I don't understand part of the instructions for
winterizing, as I don't know where things are. (See
Winterizing sheet.)
When do I have to be concerned about pipes freezing?
Can I possibly get by putting anti-freeze in just the traps
in November? (e.g. how many days of below freezing
weather before they freeze without it?)
9.   If I had an accident who would do the body work?
10. What are screws for on the walls of unit? Curtain
rods?

11. What are longer bars for on awning?

_____

12. What is the size of the foam needed for the air conditioner?

_____

13. Electric: What are breakers for? Not labeled. Why do I have fuses and breakers? Are they for different things or do different jobs?

_____

14. What has to be done with the following for maintenance?

Furnace_____

_____

Refrigerator

_____

_____

Water
Heater_____

_____

Water
Pump_____

_____

What concerns do I need to consider when in higher altitudes? At what altitude?
Derating? Gas type to use?

15. What is switch for in bedroom under water heater?

16 Does the a/c have something on the roof to keep the unit warm instead of using the furnace?

17. What are the type/size of jacks I should be buying for the slide out? Can I be shown how to use them? Where are they placed?

_____

How many?

18. Water Heater: Where is the reset button? Limit switch?
Pressure relief valve? Does bypass valve stop water from going into the hot water heater? How do I know if burner is burning yellow?
Where and what is a PC board?

Do 3 drains drain this?

Not sure I understand the water system. Is this correct?

As long as water is coming out of the faucets I can assume that there is water in the water heater? So I'm safe to turn it on then?

If there is no water in the fresh water tanks and the unit is not hooked up to water. I can burn up the water heater.

If hose is hooked up with the water off and the pump is turned on will I drain the water heater? (e.g. is there a sensor at the hook up.)

19. Can't get green light on TV to stop flashing. Something is wrong.

20. Batteries:
Type? Wet cell _____ Gel cell_____AGM _____
If Gel/AGM how are they ventilated?
Any maintenance on these batteries? e.g. Water?

How are they hooked up? Series ____ or Parallel?
_____
Is a battery charger any good to me? If so, where?

Using the inverter: How long can I safely use it?
_____
Does it take the charge from the motor battery?

_____
Can it ruin the battery?
21. Where to spray soapy water to check for LP gas leak.
22. I couldn't get the generator to start one day. I'm assuming that the batteries have to be with a full charge to start it. Is that so?
23. Which port do I use to plug in the Inverter?
24. Can't find the heat for just the top part of the cab. It looks like it is only for the floor (which gets too hot as it is) and mixed. Help!
25. Who put the plastic over the carpet? Previous owner?
26. Why is my title stating that it's for the month of March when I purchased the unit in June? I thought a title was supposed to reflect the month of purchase. Also if the unit was taken in during March and it sat on the lot in snow, that could have possibly been the reason for the rusty/frozen small back wheels on the unit. (See # 11 below).

Work to be completed by dealership. I was told that I could bring the RV back when I went south, for repairs that needed to be completed.
1. Install a TV antenna for local stations. Instructions on use.

2. Green light on TV keeps blinking even though I keep turning the timer off.

3. Adjust door with screen door. Instruct me on adjustment. e.g. where should it be for a good connection?

4. Door handle loose.

5. Bedroom lamps—short? Flicker. Second bulb doesn't come on. (I wonder if this problem is connected to the problem with the refrigerator/slide)?

6. Check seals around unit. Repair them. How do I recognize a bad seal and what has to be done to fix it?

7. No water in toilet and hose doesn't work either. I spoke with two of your service men and they both said that there should be water in the toilet and that it is probably a bad seal.

8. Bedroom/bathroom heat duct. Very little heat coming out of it. What's wrong? Floor seemed soft by register in the floor close to it.

9. Check driver's seat and get adjustments to work. Check passenger's side also.

10. Get chair in coach adjusted so it can be turned easily.

11. Small back wheels on the back are in bad shape. (My son said they are frozen.) They had not been maintained by the previous owner. As I had asked this before I purchased the RV and was assured that the back end would not drag, I feel they should replace them.

12. Get hydraulic jacks working right and grease/oil them. They only work on a flat surface and then I don't need them. They don't work with even a mild incline. I asked

the mechanic in Green Bay, Wisconsin, if they should and he said yes.

13. Drawer by entertainment center doesn't close.

14. Fresh water tank—can't get all the anti-freeze out of it. How do you get anti-freeze out of unit after it has been winterized?

15. Work black water tank valve and fresh water drain so they aren't so hard to use. Even my son had problems with this. I've put Vaseline on the black water valve, but it doesn't help much. The fresh water valve is difficult to close.

16. CO detector should be at ground level.

I haven't had the opportunity to see if the convection oven works. Can you check this?

Repairs to be paid for by Owner: Before work begins, please tell me the cost.

1. Refrigerator: I cannot get it to go on electric, only gas.

2. I couldn't get the slide to go out.

3. As I had a problem getting the generator to start please check it.

4. I would like to know what the cost of installing another outlet would be.

**Compiled after reading Gulf Stream's manual

Appendix 8: Motor Home: Items to Take.
1. Money/traveler's checks, coins, MC.
2. Music.
3. Bread machine.
4. Phone.
5. Water.
6. Bucket and brush for washing unit.
7. Spray nozzle for hose.
8. Electric cord.
9. Art and craft supplies.
10. Dishes/silverware/utensils/knives/sauce & frying pans, dishcloths & towels.
11. Neti Pot.
12. Silver polishing cloth.
13. Air filter machine/new filter as necessary.
14. Ceramic heater/space heater.
15. Kneeling pad.
16. Edward D Jones info.
17. Tax information.
18. Ice bag.
19. FM system.
20. Battery charger.
21. Night light.
22. Nail brush.
23. Bread board.
24. CD map and other computer CD's.
25. Laptop/printer/paper/floppies or Work CD-RW's.
26. Exercise pad.
27. Small table.
28. Jewelry.
29. Batteries for aids and CB.
30. Bike/helmet/locks/bungee cords.
31. Grill.
32. Laundry detergent and bounce (sm. amount).
33. All keys necessary.

34. Bread knife.
35. Rags.
36. Leather coat.
37. Stick pins.
38. Kleenex.
39. Lawn chairs.
40. Trailer Life.
41. Bible/Strongs/notebooks/tapes.
42. Camera and batteries.
43. Massager.
44. Ballet slippers.
45. Swimsuit, sandals and cover-up.
46. Chemicals for RV.
47. Tea pot/coffee pot.
48. Afghans.
49. Cuddle Ewe?
50. Night light.
51. Bed foam pads/blankets/pillows/sheets &
    cases/towels and washrags.
52. Bathroom and kitchen stuff.
53. Golf clubs.
54. Envelopes for receipts.
55. Small amount of gas in Honda.
56. New Hallmark date book.
57. Little red notebook and address book.
58. Card making stuff.
59. Pieces of carpet if I have any.
60. Safe.
61. Tools/vice grip/tire covers/ tire pressure
    gauge/barometer w/temp gauge.
62. Christmas decorations when needed.
63. Warm jacket/mittens/hat.
64. Small lamp.
65. Recipes/card file.
66. Lawn chairs: light weight ones.
67. Level.

68. Kitchen supplies like Windex.
69. Carpet pieces for outside.
70. Distiller as required.
71. Jacks for slide, as required.
72. Hedge apples to fight bugs.
73. Pepper spray.
74. Umbrella and rain gear.
75. Books + The Next Exit and atlas.

Appendix 9: Quick Reference for Manual.

For Generator: Fleming Sales, 2101 Industrial Pkwy, Elkhart, 219-295-0234.
For Furnace: (Suburban) RV America Inc. 2010 Cassopolis, 219 264-9621.
For Refrigerator; (Domestic) LaGrange, In. See Manual for number.

Appendix 10: RV/Car Care.
Do Maintenance on RV and Car.
1. Oil change, etc.
2. Spray all moveable parts with silicone.
3. Check transmission fluid in hydraulics.
4. Put DW-40 where needed, don't forget CRV tow bar.
5. Check tire pressure, 80 in back 75 in front.
6. Check water in all batteries.
7. Have roof cleaned and all seals checked.
8. See list of repairs.
9. Side mirrors.
10. Weather stripping.
11. Generator maintenance.
12. Mold under shower.

Shopping Cart   Help   Contact Us   Mem

Resources

Home + Quick Search

Alphabetical Listing

Journals by Subject

For Authors

For Librarians

FAQs

My Account

My Files

SARA (Contents Alerting)

Support Information

Library Recommendation Form

Linking Options

Article

Back To: Mai

Click here to ı

Amyotrophic Lateral Sclerosis and Other Motor Neuron Disorders

Publisher: Taylor & Francis Health Sciences, part of the Taylor & Francis Group

Issue: Volume 4, Number 3 / September 2003

Pages: 136 - 143

URL: Linking Options

DOI: 10.1080/14660820310011250

Full Text Acc

Full Text Secu

The full text of subscribers. To

○ Subscribe

○ Add this it
for purcha

○ Purchase

○ Log in to v

Amyotrophic lateral sclerosis: A review of current concepts

Michael Strong [A1] and Jeffrey Rosenfeld [A2]

[A1] The Department of Clinical Neurological Sciences The University of Western Ontario London Canada

[A2] The Carolinas Neuromuscular/ALS-MDA Center Carolinas Medical Center Charlotte North Carolina

Abstract:

Amyotrophic lateral sclerosis (ALS), once thought to be a rare neurodegenerative disease, affects between 1.2 and 1.8/100,000 individuals. This age-dependent disorder, similar to other major neurological disorders of the aging population (Alzheimer's and Parkinson's disease) is increasing in incidence at a rate which cannot be accounted for by population aging alone. Multiple clinical variants of ALS are now recognized which are associated with a spectrum of clinical outcomes from aggressive to rather indolent. Three variants of ALS are generally accepted, including the western Pacific type (often associated with dementia), familial (the majority of which are autosomal dominant in their inheritance) and classic sporadic ALS. Considerable biological heterogeneity underlies the disease process of ALS. By the time ALS is clinically evident, derangements at the cellular level in ALS are extensive and include alterations in the cytoskeleton, mitochondrial function, microglial activation, and the metabolism of reactive oxygenating species and glutamate. Our understanding of the genetic aspects of the disease continues to expand. These observations have led to the suggestion that multiple distinct etiologies may be responsible. Recent advances have also included the observation that cognitive decline may be present in a population of patients not previously recognised. Significant advances in both symptomatic and adjunctive therapy have resulted in prolonged quality and duration of life.

Keywords:

Brief explanation of the differences
between ALS and PBP

Amyotrophic lateral sclerosis (a-mi-oh-TROH-fik LAT-ur-ul skluh-ROH-sis), or ALS, is a serious neurological disease that causes muscle weakness, disability and eventually death. ALS is often called Lou Gehrig's disease, after the famous baseball player who was diagnosed with it in 1939. In the U.S., ALS and motor neuron disease (MND) are sometimes used interchangeably. Worldwide, ALS occurs in 1 to 3 people per 100,000. In the vast majority of cases — 90 to 95 percent — doctors don't yet know why ALS occurs. About 5 to 10 percent of ALS cases are inherited. ALS often begins with muscle twitching and weakness in an arm or leg, or with slurring of speech. Eventually, ALS affects your ability to control the muscles needed to move, speak, eat and breathe. The disease frequently begins in your hands, feet or limbs, and then spreads to other parts of your body. As the disease advances, your muscles become progressively weaker until they're paralyzed. It eventually affects chewing, swallowing, speaking and breathing.

PBP

This search was completed August 2011. The results are still the same as you can see. "We're sorry, your search for **"Progressive Bulbar Palsy"** returned no results." My empirical knowledge, which was acquired while living this story and from various medical doctors, shows that the disease process for PBP is the opposite of ALS. Whereas ALS starts in the extremities and gradually proceeds toward the trunk of the body, PBP starts in the trunk of the body and proceeds outward toward the limbs. Expected survival rate with PBP is three to five years. ALS expected survival rate varies. Data collected 2011 from www.mayo.com

271.

The Carolee Collectables
by Carolee O'Neill

Goodie RudeShoes: Series One, children 5-100.
Billy BitterBetter: Series Two, children 5-100.
Granny NeatFreak: children 4-100.
The Mouse House: children 4-100.
That Secret Part of Me: children 3 to 100.
From Silly to Sinister, Short Stories.
Book One and Two.
For teens to mature adults.
Navigating the Potholes of Life:
Fiction, adventure, comedy, drama
for teens and adults.
A Reason to Dream:
Fiction based on a true story
for teens and adults.
Three versions of the following book.
The Graduation: A stand-alone novel
with suspense, drama and humor
for teens and adults.
The Graduation with Study Guide
for parents with teens, teens and adults.
The Graduation Study Guide.
for the person who prefers a separate copy.
With God in Mind.
Thought provoking prose.
for teens and adults.

caroleeagain1934@gmail.com
http://books2c4kids.com
Carolee's books are available as paperbacks and as ebooks.
Thank you for your interest in my work.

Chocolate

Carolee O'Neill